Only men already under sentence of death are offered the chance to become Ion Warriors—no one else would be willing to make that terrible choice, and to endure the agony of ion transformation. There are times when Dam Stormdragon sees the simplicity of death as a blissful alternative. But Dam is a fighter, born on a brave Colony planet, and the Terran masters will never break his spirit. If the Terrans were more attentive, they might notice that most of the invincible Ion Warriors are from the Colonies . . . and Dam is not the only one with a score to settle.

Another novel of thrilling science fiction adventure from the author of PATTERNS OF CHAOS.

Other ACE books by Colin Kapp:

PATTERNS OF CHAOS

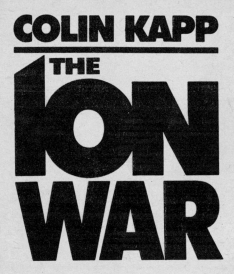

COLIN KAPP
THE ION WAR

ace books
A Division of Charter Communications Inc.
A GROSSET & DUNLAP COMPANY
360 Park Avenue South
New York, New York 10010

THE ION WAR

Copyright © 1978 by Colin Kapp

An ACE Book

Cover art by Ken Barr

First Ace Printing: October 1978

Printed in U.S.A.

CHAPTER I

Dam Stormdragon brought the water-sled expertly round to the mooring pole, killed the engine, and used his powerful muscles to steady the craft while Tetri jumped the half meter from the pier to the sled's deck. When she was safely seated he revived the turbine and let the wash of the jets build before he cast free and made a long, slow arc back to the centre of the canal.

"And where would Tetri like to go this evening?" he teased.

"You know perfectly well! To the Water Forest—you promised!" Her voice was nearly lost beneath the turbine's roar. "But we've got to be home by twenty-seven hours for the farewell party. Senator Anrouse is guest of honour."

"Let's hope he doesn't make us late for blast-off with one of his interminable speeches."

They both laughed as Dam pushed the water-sled swiftly through the waters of the canal. The passage of the craft woke tinkling echoes from stone-blocked recesses in the banks, and the creamy wake washed high against the corners of the old steps. It was nearing the end of first-light, and the waterways were nearly deserted: already Castalia's great moon was beginning to soften the shadows under the bridges; soon the great star-banks of the Hub would take upon themselves the chore of providing second-light, relegating the dizzy moon to a mere diversion in the sky.

Coming to the river, they turned upstream; here the swell so bounced the little sled that Dam was forced to reduce speed and pay heed to the dictates of the tide. This compromise between the forces of nature and his own skill and the power of his engines was a challenge he relished. Tetri relaxed and leaned back, enjoying the sight of his strong face with its comprehending eyes as he concentrated on navigating through the difficult currents to reach the narrower channels leading to the Water Forest. Both were aware that this might be their last time together.

The super-abundance of water on Castalia made natural fountains commonplace, but nowhere was there such a display as the Water Forest could provide; especially in the wake of the moon when the great subterranean tides hurled water upwards through a plain of lightly-fragmented bedrock, creating whole an ephemeral landscape sculptured from living water. Dam had been born on the Forest's edge; he knew the ways of the waters better than many of the guides. Now, with skillful hands at the sled's controls, he took the craft through and around the graves of sparkling silver 'trees', where the fountains spun faster and purer and more mobile than any who had not seen them could possibly have believed. The great ranks of the stars above contributed a billion scintillating points of light which were then refracted by the flying spray, arching the whole scene with a rainbow canopy which touched fringes of color into every dancing water-wraith.

Spray-drenched but enthralled, Tetri could not remember ever having enjoyed the forest so much. She suspected Dam must have taken her through some of his private places, places he normally reserved for himself. Finally they drew in at one of the rest-cabins and luxuriated in soft towels, soft music, and sweet wines until their clothes had been dried and returned to them. Then it was time to set off for Tetri's home and the last farewells before the trip to Terra.

As he pushed the sled through the slumbering waters, Dam grew gradually more silent and reflective. Tetri could guess what was on his mind, and he confirmed it by gazing for a long time at the bright star-banks.

"They say that on Terra you can see only a millionth of the stars we see on Castalia."

"Don't be silly!" she told him. "That would mean half of each day would be completely dark. Who would bother to evolve in a place like that?"

They both laughed, but the laughter soon died from his lips and his dark mood continued to grow, until finally: "What's worrying you, Dam? Always when you've spaced before you've enjoyed every second of it. What's so different about going to Terra?"

He was apologetic for his withdrawal. "I don't know. Perhaps it's the idea of it being the mother-planet. It gives it a significance it doesn't deserve. Truth to tell, Tetri, I'm afraid of Terra."

"Afraid?" She was incredulous. "You're a

spacer and a Space Army officer. Tomorrow you join my father for a tour of duty with the Terran Spaceforce—the greatest armed force the galaxy has ever known. Isn't that what you've always wanted?''

"You make it sound as if armed force had a sort of virtue in its own right. It oughtn't to be that way, Tetri. It's the purpose for which you use those arms that counts. What scares me about Terra is that I don't know what her motives are."

"Still, it isn't like you be so serious."

"Sorry, Tetri, it's not your cross." He grinned suddenly, and in an instant it seemed as if the matter was forgotten.

From the banks of the canal the terraced slopes, softened with shrubs, ran upwards as if to form a green cushion on which rested the house of Dimede—Tetri's home. Under the gentle, shadowless illumination of second-light they dawdled up the random paths between the terraces, with many a diversion so that they might marvel at the phosphorescent fish that swam in the ornate pools and leaped the little waterfalls, like streaks of burnished copper. Above them, the farewell party had already begun; the windows open to the clement air allowed bright shafts of melody to spill out across the hill. They hurried the latter part of the way, to be greeted by Tetri's mother and ushered into a circle of laughing friends who teased them about their dalliance.

"Oh, Dam . . ." Stormdragon was suddenly called from the party by Colonel Dimede, who was Tetri's father and who would also be his commanding officer on the year-long tithe-loan trip to Terra.

"Sorry to drag you away, Dam. There's somebody wants to meet you before the party gets too strong. Do you know Senator Anrouse?"

"I know *of* him; we scarcely move in the same circles," said Dam mischievously.

"Nevertheless, he's been following your career with interest. It was his recommendation, based on your prior academic performance, that helped get you into the space academy, and I think you justified his faith when you won the top-graduate award."

Dam followed the colonel into the library, there to face the personage whose face was otherwise familiar to him only from news-cast interviews. His first impression was one of mild shock at discovering the senator was not the larger-than-life figure his imagination had painted.

"Senator Anrouse—may I present Major Stormdragon, a member of my flight-staff and a friend of my daughter."

"I'd have thought all of your flight staff would have been friends of the charming Tetri—given half the opportunity," said Anrouse, smiling and rising from his chair. "Glad to make your acquaintance, Stormdragon! The name's not unknown to me. I served under your father in the Vilion campaign."

"He often spoke of you, sir."

"And now you've followed his ion-trails into space, eh? Can't say I blame you. If I'd my youth again I'd be right out there with you. How do you feel about a year's tithe-loan to Terra?"

"Apprehensive," said Dam honestly.

Anrouse scowled slightly. "Don't tell me you object to Terran service?"

"I don't object to any service. But I do have reservations about the uses to which Terra puts her arms."

"Specifically?"

"Rigon, Zino, and Ames' World. Three Hub planets wasted because of dissension with the mother-planet."

Anrouse was examining the major's face carefully.

"You're well informed, Dam. Far better than I'd thought. Information for such a view is not generally available. Let that be one of the strengths you take with you—the impressions you're given are not necessarily true. Above all things, preserve an open mind."

"Thank you, sir!" Dam presumed the interview was at a close. He turned to go, but Anrouse motioned for him to remain, while looking meaningfully at Colonel Dimede, who discreetly picked up a tray of empty goblets and excused himself.

"Before you go, Dam, there's something I want to say to you in confidence."

"Sir?"

"Despite what you may think, your choice for inclusion on the tithe-loan trip to Terra was no accident. The reasons will not become apparent to you for some time, but they were the result of much careful consideration. Think of that when the going gets tough. It may help you through."

"I'll bear it in mind, sir," Dam said, mystified.

"Good! And in return for that I'll give you an assurance of my own. We in the government are not unmindful of what happened to Rigon, Zino and Ames' World. After all, we have far more in common with our Hub neighbours than we have with the mother-planet; the Hub would not have been colonized at all except that the fathers of the Exodus were dissidents on Terra. But neither shall we allow the fate of those three worlds to be shared by Castalia if we can possibly avoid it. Therefore we must move carefully, in our own way and in our own time. Take heart, Dam. We may not appear to share your spirit of rebellion, but I assure you we do—and we shall win.''

At that point Colonel Dimede returned with a new tray of goblets and they drank a solemn toast to Castalia that was followed by pleasant conversation until Tetri came and scolded them for both their sobriety and their absence from the party.

Senator Anrouse's speech during supper was without reference to a possible schism between Terra and Castalia. Both the colonel and Dam were congratulated on having been selected to serve with the great army of the mother-planet, and hopes were extended for their safe return. This was Anrouse the politician, operating with polished phrases rich in rhetoric but empty of meaning. Suddenly Dam began to appreciate the dual nature of the man and to understand a little about how such an apparently shallow character commanded so much influence in the Castalian senate. Neither encounter, however, did anything to convince Dam that the Castalian government was in any way prepared or able to challenge the yoke of Terra.

After that, the party grew wild, with the sparkling music rising to new heights of rhythm and fury which wound gradually up to the great crescendo dances, leaving them all happily exhausted. Then, as the creeping reds and golds of first-light began to occupy the sky, Dam and Tetri crept out to the terraced garden for a soft farewell which was perhaps also a goodbye; they knew that a year's separation would change them both, that the old liaison might never be renewed. Finally Dam, cloak draped casually over his shoulder and ignoring the chilly dampness of the early dew, set off with an apparent air of jauntiness towards his sled and the first leg of his journey toward the mother planet of mankind.

CHAPTER II

Liam Liam was having a bad day. The Z-ship *Starbucket*, painstakingly disguised as a charter tramp to give him professional cover, was picked up by a Terran ship-chain after his course vectors had already made it clear that Liam's intention was to make planetfall on Sette; unable to protest that he had actually been *en route* to some other world, Liam had ordered his engines cut and was now waiting the arrival of a pinnace from the armed Terran cruiser which had secured his 'arrest'.

Had the cruiser been alone Liam could have eliminated it with the weaponry concealed in the Z-ship's modified hull. The presence of the other ships in the chain, however, was a factor he could not surmount: and even though he might have forced an escape, this would have revealed the strength of his hand, which he was not prepared to do. The importance of his arrival on Sette could not be over-told, and now his one hope of reaching the planet lay in the possibility of bluffing his way through the impending confrontation.

As the pinnace moved in on *Starbucket* Liam warily gauged its velocity and angle of approach. For all the careful camouflage, had the pinnace passed directly behind his stern nothing could have concealed the fact that what looked like an old tramp was equipped with modern engines larger and more powerful than those of the pinnace's mother ship.

Fortunately the pinnace approached from the side, and the aimless spiral which had been imparted to the *Starbucket's* motion gave the on-coming pilot too much to think about for him to have time to study the tramp too closely.

After much searching for compatible terminations to the space-transfer tube, the Terran party finally gained access. They traversed the greasy, cluttered corridors with an air of affronted distaste, and their nostrils curled in rebellion when they were finally shown into Liam's untidy stateroom and encountered the pungent odors emanating from the captain's pipe.

"Captain Liam?" The Terran officer had meant to be aggressive and abrupt, but his eyes were on the nicotine-stained air vent that should have been exchanging the cabin's malodorous atmosphere with air fit to breathe; the entire grate was plugged with cotton waste.

"At your service, Major!" Liam looked every centimeter the part he played: slack, middle-aged, with a bulbous nose and a genial face lined and warted by a lifetime's exposure to the radiations of space.

The officer visibly pulled himself together. "Captain Liam, you have brought your vessel into a sector of space into which entry is prohibited by Space-emergency Ordinance."

"Oh?" said Liam. "What's the emergency? Perhaps I can help?"

"I don't think you understand me. The emergency lies on the planetary territory of Sette. Therefore these space approaches are out of bounds to all save military craft."

"But if they've an emergency on Sette, surely any sort of spacecraft could be of help?"

"Not in this case. Their emergency is an insurrection."

"Then it is helpful that I'm a neutral. Perhaps I can talk some sense into them. Insurrections are bad for trade, you understand?"

"Captain Liam!" The Terran officer was growing increasingly intolerant with the trend of the conversation. "I don't seem to be getting through to you. I'll make it plain. There is no chance of your being allowed to make planetfall on Sette. If you wish to avoid having your ship confiscated, you'll leave as fast as your burners will drive you."

"I'd go with pleasure, Major. But there's a snag. A cargo awaits me on Sette, and with the contract price I can afford to buy the fuel to take me away again. Forbid me my cargo, and it's here I must stay. It's difficult, you understand?"

"Stay? Out of the question! I warn you, Captain, get this hulk out of these approaches, or I'll be forced to confiscate it."

"That might be a solution," said Liam thoughtfully. "I've insurances covering such a contingency, and the old bucket's useless to me stuck here. But that won't get rid of it. I suppose you wouldn't consider towing us to the nearest free-port?"

The officer glanced at one of his companions, who shrugged. "Sangria on Maroc is the nearest—ninety light-years."

"Space!" The officer turned back to Liam, wrinkling his nose at the fume from the captain's pipe. "Do you realize how long that would take at towing rate?"

"About seven years, I should think," said Liam philosophically, beginning to close down his control panels with an air of finality. "I said it was difficult. Seems best if we just sit here until the insurrection's over."

"Wait!" The officer was consulting with his colleagues. "You do have enough fuel at least to reach Sette?"

"Only because the good Lord made it downhill all the way."

"Then you've twenty-four hours to make planetfall and be offworld again. If you're still around after that deadline we'll save the shipbreakers the job of having to delouse this crawling meat-can before dismantling. Do I make myself perfectly clear?"

"I shall remember you to the end of my days," said Liam Liam sincerely. "Shall we drink to that?"

The officer looked at the cut-down bottles, caked with grime, that Liam proffered as glasses for the toast, and ordered his party to make a quick return to the pinnace. He was shaking his head sadly as he made his final exit.

Watching the pinnace blast away, Liam spat expressively into a fire point.

"Indeed I'll remember you, you Terran bastard! Sette was a very pleasant world: now it's a battlefield; six tenths of the arable land defoliated and poisoned, nearly half its former population murdered. But remembrance isn't forgiveness, you understand?''

He was speaking reflectively but his pilot-navigator, Euken Tor, who had followed the whole of the preceding conversation over the intercom, and who had now come for further orders, nodded in grim affirmation.

"How do we play it, Skipper?"

"Carry on like we were limping, Euk. Make planetfall at Wanderplas. Then make sure everything's tuned for a fast departure. I doubt if it's going to be as easy to get out as it was to get in."

"How do you compute that?"

"The obvious thing to do with an unwanted tramp is to leave it parked in orbit. For some reason, that was not acceptable. It suggests the Terrans have a special operation going, and they don't want observers. That ties in with our own information. It's this special operation I came to see, and if it's what I think it is, they'll not want me alive to tell the tale. So when we leave, it is like a bat out of hell, you understand?"

Euken nodded. "Do you want any support on the ground?"

"I think not. Jon Rakel should have the arrangements already complete. Your job is to get me out through the ship-chain once I've got what I came for, you understand?"

"Understood and noted, Skip." Euken wandered off in the direction of the flight bridge, his casual mien belying the fact that his every action had a precalculated purpose. One of the best space navigators in all the Hub fleets, he had fully adapted his talents to the apparently minor role of piloting the little Z-ship. Like Liam Liam, he had personal reasons for dedicating himself to the fight against Terra.

At Wanderplas spaceport on Sette, a fast, tracked vehicle was waiting for Liam by the landing pads. In the driving seat Jon Rakel himself, since the last pogrom almost the sole commander of Sette Combined Resistance Forces, greeted Liam thankfully. The two men had enjoyed many years of mutual respect.

"I was afraid you wouldn't get through, Liam."

"Heh! They may have more ships and more guns, but Liam Liam has his own secret weapon, you understand? He bores them into submission."

They both laughed, and Rakel put the vehicle swiftly through the approach roads of the spaceport complex; but Rakel's laughter was taut, and stress and weariness lined his face. Presumably for reasons of future convenience, the Terran anti-insurgent strikes had left the spaceport undisturbed, but once they reached the surrounding township the substantial damage caused by selective space bombing was brutally obvious. Under the pretext of eliminating 'terrorist cells' the population of Sette was being shown the terrible price they must pay for attempting to break the ties with the mother planet. Here the sad stories of Rigon, Zino, and Ames' World were being repeated over again.

As they headed into open country, now bitterly desolate from the poisonous dusting which permitted only the hardiest grasses to survive, Liam recovered from the depression which the scene had induced, and brought his mind back to the problems ahead.

"You'd better bring me up to date, Jon. The messages I received weren't specific."

"Frankly, I think we're seeing what they saw on Rigon just before the end. We built some virtually impregnable command-points on Sette, emplacements that the Terrans couldn't crack by any conventional means. They were the basis of our war plans; we thought the Terrans would have had to withdraw because of the length of their supply lines. But instead they've brought in a special unit which can crack a command-point as easily as you or I can crack a nut."

"What's special about tactical nukes?"

"No, not nuclear: our command-points are *hardened*, I tell you; commando."

"Commando?" Liam was surprised. "Surely . . ."

Rakel cut in swiftly. "These are special—very special. I don't like to think about who they are or how they operate, but they're a hundred percent effective. If they continue their present pattern, there won't be any effective resistance on Sette inside six months."

Liam whistled with surprise. "Well, if there's a way to beat the bastards, we'll find it."

"Listen to me, Liam! If there was an easy answer, we'd already have found it. There isn't. Strictly between ourselves, Sette is already finished. I wish to God I could say otherwise. I asked you here to analyse this thing that they're using against us, and to take that knowledge back to the rest of the Hub. Then our sacrifice won't have been quite in vain. With luck perhaps you'll have time enough to prepare against it before the next planet's turn comes."

"If anyone else except Jon Rakel had said that to me, I'd have said his nerve was going."

"It's not a question of nerve. With strong command-points, even if we couldn't win at least we couldn't entirely lose. Against all reprisals we always had the psychological assurance that some of us would survive and that we could hold the planet. Now the Terrans can take any command-point as and when they choose, and the weight of reprisals must be viewed against reality. It's the choice between retaining some indigenous population—albeit as slaves—or none at all."

"You mean capitulation?" Liam handled the word as though it was newly minted and of doubtful origin.

"Rigon and Zino fought to the last. Both were sterilized with neutron bombs, and Ames' World is scarcely better off. Currently Sette has a population of around five hundred million. In the present situation, how many of them am I justified in losing before I admit I'm unable to defend the rest?"

"That's the sort of dilemma no man should face alone, you understand? Show me what you want, Jon. Then let my counsel weigh in your decision."

"That's why I asked for you to come personally, Liam. I know how to gauge the strength of the things you say. In the name of Humanity, whatever decision's made, it mustn't be the wrong one."

CHAPTER III

After leaving Tetri, Dam went first to his home near the Water Forest to don his uniform and to pick-up a few personal belongings. Then he set off for the Space Army landing pads, with one last regretful look at the forest fountains now misted and subdued and reflecting his own heaviness of heart. Soon he was back on the river, fighting to control the bucking sled in the strong swell, and for the very first time hating the sight of the tall spacecraft standing beside the river's mouth, half mist-shrouded and half reaching for the stars.

The ship assigned to the tithe-loan mission was the *Starspite*, one of the newest and best equipped cruisers the Castalian Space Army possessed. Dam achieved his goal of reporting for duty well before Colonel Dimede came aboard; though he had been a privileged guest at Dimede's house, the colonel was now his commanding officer, and all such privilege belonged to a time that had passed. The first hours were busy with flight preparation, and by the time of the colonel's arrival all the final checks and parades had been readied. Dimede returned

Dam's salute with a commendation on his efficiency, but never a trace of recognition passed between their eyes.

It was a trip of thirty thousand light-years from the Hub to the star called Sol. This immense distance was to be covered in ten leaps into and out of tachyon space, three thousand light-years at a stride. Time in T-space, combined with the building up of entry-velocities and the essential real-space navigation periods between the jumps, gave a projected journey time of thirty-five days, and this schedule Dam was determined to keep. Perhaps in compensation for his lack of enthusiasm for the object of the trip, he threw himself into his work with a single-minded intensity that permitted him little relaxation. What spare time he did have he spent in the libary and the viewing theater, absorbing every scrap of information he could find about Terra. Colonel Dimede noted his absolute dedication unhappily, but didn't comment.

For the major part of the journey they had space to themselves, and navigational chores consisted merely of position fixing and course calculations for the next tachyon jump. Nine thousand light years from Sol, however, they began to encounter Terran ship-chains, which policed an unbelievably large radius around the Terran sun and very ably intercepted the passage of the line cruiser speeding in from the Hub. A pattern of challenges and enforced waiting for clearance, coupled with having to re-cast course calculation to take the ship through 'permitted' movement channels, completely destroyed Dam's journey schedule. It also gave him the impression that the mother planet must be suffering from a galaxy-sized persecution mania.

In particular, the directing of the *Starspite* through limited-movement channels, when Dam knew perfectly well there were light-years between them and the nearest other vessel, irked him considerably. He spent many off-duty hours at the star maps before he began to suspect that the real purpose of such diversions was to keep the *Starspite* away from several large sectors of space, each of which he found to contain at least one world which could not be expected to suffer Terran dominance gladly. Whether the *Starspite* was being kept out of regions where punitive reprisals were taking place, or whether rebellious forces were sweeping these sectors, he could only speculate; but he silently rejoiced that the Terrans apparently had something concrete to be nervous about.

Their eventual entry into the Solar system brought a massive surprise. Never before had Dam even imagined a concentration of spacecraft such as that which thronged this closed area of space. The complications of the traffic regulations were such that they were forced to take on a pilot to assist navigation through the orbital transfer routines made even more wretched with rules and penalties and dogma beyond belief. Dam shadowed the pilot every instant and copied every instruction into the computer banks for future reference. Dam was one of the most highly qualified officers in the Castalian spaceforce and bitterly resented the imposition of the ridiculous disciplines which overrode his expertise and took his powers of discretion away from him.

When the *Starspite* finally achieved parking orbit around Terra Colonel Dimede was ferried down to meet his new commander, leaving Dam as duty officer in charge of the ship. Dam accepted the post sourly, wondering how he was going to be able to contain his anger and frustration through a whole year of enforced tithe service. The crew sensed his mood and adopted it also, and Dam reigned in temporary command of one of the unhappiest ships in Castalia's entire Space Army.

He was not left long to brood, however. The colonel could scarcely have made planetfall before a pinnace arrived with official Terran visitors aboard.

"Port Marshal Segger." The tall officer who emerged through the space-lock introduced himself.

This was Dam's first contact with a Terran officer in the flesh. He was unpleasantly surprised by the sallowness of the man's complexion and the hideous pock-marks in his flesh. The uniform, too, with its grim authoritarian greyness, spoke of a joyless dedication.

"Major Stormdragon, officer-commanding in the absence of Colonel Dimede," said Dam, making a clumsy attempt to return the awkward Terran salute. "Did you not receive word that Colonel Dimede had already made planetfall?"

"I'm well aware of the colonel's whereabouts," Segger replied with a thin-lipped smile. "But there are formalities which can be concluded in his absence. I'm here for the purpose of vetting your security. Shall we go to your office, Major."

Biting his lip, Dam led the way, and the port marshal and his two aides followed hawkishly. Dam found them seats at the chart table, and called for refreshments to be sent.

"You must explain to me what you mean by

security," he said to Seggar. "I'd have thought there were few things more secure than a space-cruiser in parking orbit."

"I wasn't referring to external security. I was speaking of security within the ship—perhaps even within the minds of the officers and crew themselves."

"Then that's easily settled. The entire craft is manned by Castalian Space Army regulars. Their loyalty is subject to no doubt."

"Loyalty to whom?" asked Segger. "That's the key question."

Dam found it hard to control his annoyance. "They're loyal to their service, and their service demands part of their duty be performed through transfer of allegiance to Terra. Inboard security is my responsibility, and I am happy with the situation as it stands."

"But I am not," said Segger crisply. "At least, not until I've satisfied myself on the point. I want all your personnel records, including your own and Colonel Dimede's."

"Even if I agreed, I've no authority to make them available to you."

"But I have the authority to require you to surrender them, Major." Segger laid a piece of paper on the table. "That's a Command Order, which you may not refuse. Now produce the records, and leave us alone with them until we send for you."

Seething with a scarcely concealable anger, Dam turned on the communicator, placed the paper on the scanning pad, and picked up the handset.

"Connect with Lieutenant Corda, immediately."

The screen lit up with the face of Soo Corda, the ship's legal officer. She smiled drowsily as though she had been awakened from a deep sleep.

"What's on your mind, Dam?"

"I've been presented with a Terran Command Order requiring me to release our confidential personnel records for inspection. Need I comply?"

She looked at the image transmitted from the scanning pad for a few moments, with an increasing frown coming across her brow. "I'm afraid you must, Dam. This has a legal status conferred by our own government under Space Convention agreements. For us it has the force of law."

"That's what I was afraid of," said Dam. "Thanks anyway."

He cut the connection and turned back to Segger. "You win, Marshal!"

"I always do," said Segger flatly, without a trace of triumph in his voice.

Dam arranged for the necessary records to be obtained, then went to the flight-bridge, which was relatively inactive while the *Starspite* was parked. Here he busied himself with cleaning up the computer information for the orbital transfers into and out of the Solar system. He had come to Terra hating the whole concept of tithe-service; nothing so far had modified his views, and to his original misgivings had now been added a growing detestation of the Terrans themselves. He was beginning to fear that the coming year would change him even more than Tetri had suggested.

Four hours later that he was summoned back to his office. The records had been sorted into orderly piles, and pads of notes, apparently culled from them, were stacked high in front of the aids. Only one record remained in front of the port marshal, and that was Dam's own.

"Sit down, Major. You'll be pleased to know we are satisfied with what we find. So satisfied that I suspect Hub Intelligence has been more than usually diligent in anticipating our thoughts on the matter. I've only a few questions to ask, and these concern yourself."

"Me?" Dam was genuinely surprised.

"Your father was in the Vilion campaign, was he not?"

"So I believe. I remember him speaking of it."

"Did he ever discuss the politics behind the Vilion insurrection?"

"If he did," said Dam, "it's beyond my recollection. I was only eleven when he died."

"I see." Segger wrote something on a pad. "And how well do you know Senator Anrouse?"

"I've spoken to him once only—over a glass of wine. Otherwise we've never met. Where the hell is all this leading?"

"Do you always answer questions so belligerently?"

"Only when they're stupid ones. What is the possible relevance between a cocktail chat and my security arrangements for this ship?"

The port marshal studied him carefully for a few seconds. "Possibly none. For the moment I'll give you the benefit of the doubt." He glanced at his aides. "Well, gentlemen, I think that concludes our examination. If anything further comes to light we'll communicate with Colonel Dimede through the usual channels. And Major . . ."

"Marshal?" Dam looked up, struck by the sudden ice in the man's tone.

"Am I to take it that you object to Terran service?"

"I know very little about Terran service. I've only just arrived. But I tend to take things as I find them. So far I've encountered nothing but frustration and unwarranted suspicion. Perhaps tomorrow will be different."

"A circumspect answer, and one you'll do well to remember. Believe me, Stormdragon, you certainly live up to your reputation for outspokenness. It's a habit you would be advised to curb while on the Rim."

CHAPTER IV

In a field depot roughly camouflaged beneath an edge of sickly trees, Jon Rakel had a flier waiting. Liam was impressed by the toughncss and efficiency of the crew manning the depot and their obvious respect for the man who now bore sole command responsibility: but they were war-weary men, and every eye was haunted by the specter of defeat.

Watching his chronometer anxiously, Rakel waited until the last vestiges of light had faded from the sky before he nosed the craft out from its precarious hangar and set off into the night sky. Once airborne, he switched to a pre-set instrumented course and relaxed back in the seat.

"Where are we headed?" asked Liam.

"One of our command-points, Base 22. It has deep shelters which can withstand nuclear attack, more firepower than a regiment, and a Benedict force-field straight off a class-ten space dreadnought. We expect to lose Base 22 tonight."

"A fatalistic prediction."

"No, a realistic prediction. Such situations aren't new to us."

"Why tonight?"

"The Terrans aren't at all subtle about how they plan their attacks: they started with the most northerly of our command-points and they've been working their way systematically down the map at four day intervals. Tonight it's Base 22's turn. I think they're trying to make the point that even though we know where and when the next blow will fall, there's nothing we can do about it."

"That is what bothers me," said Liam. "If you know when and where an attack will come, why can't you mount a defense against it?"

"You won't understand until you've seen it with your own eyes." Rakel's voice sounded hollow against the background of the engine's song. "How do you mount a defense against ghosts?"

"Ghosts?"

"Something akin to. Whatever they are, they're certainly not substantial."

"Yet they can fight?"

"With radiation weapons always. Lasers, electron rifles, heat-projectors—all that class of stuff. And nothing stops them. They'll walk straight through any sort of weaponfire we can throw at them. They're uncanny—and very deadly."

"How many of these 'ghosts' are there?"

"One ship, about a dozen ghosts."

"This is incredible, you understand? Are you telling me you're likely to lose Sette because of a dozen ghosts?"

"I'm not telling you anything, Liam. I simply want you to see for yourself. If you can give us any ideas that might offer a shred of hope, we'll try them. We've exhausted every approach we know."

Once in the high stratosphere the flier hit mach three and stayed there for nearly an hour before suddenly cutting velocity to follow a gentle descent path, the later stage of which was controlled from the ground. The complexity and precision of the data exchange was sufficient to assure Liam that the defenders still retained a high level of technical competence despite the near totality of their 'war.' That made it all the more difficult to understand Rakel's acceptance of the idea that a dozen ghosts of whatever caliber could decide the fate of Sette. He reserved his judgment, however, having known Jon long enough to understand that a problem which baffled him was a problem indeed.

A short distance above the ground Rakel switched to hover mode and passed Liam a night-scope. With this the agent was able to peer down on what seemed to be the ruins of a city sprawled over the dome of a low hill.

"Base 22," explained Rakel. "Mainly underground. If you follow the skyline you'll see a trace of the Benedict forcefield. It's a full ten microns thick; a crashing spacecraft couldn't dent it."

"I see it. Does it have windows?"

"Five in all, synchronized with our weaponfire. But all the gunnery positions are so well bunkered that anything penetrating a window could destroy no more than the weapons positioned directly beneath."

"Which by all normal reckoning is as impenetrable as you can get."

"So we'd hoped," said Rakel sourly.

Their landing target was a concrete pad close to a pair of massive fortified doors that opened at their approach. For the single moment in which the flier taxied through a window was created in the Benedict field to permit their passage. Instantly upon the craft having cleared the field the window was withdrawn and again the impenetrable field hugged the whole complex safely within its shell of energy.

From the vast vehicle bay they had entered, they were conducted swiftly down through many levels to a control center where ranked screens permitted comprehensive visual monitoring of both the interior and exterior of Base 22. Liam was introduced to the officer in command of the base, who had already evolved plans for Liam's escape in the event that the coming attack followed its assumed course. Against the possibility that events might take an even worse course, Liam was provided with an electron rifle and placed in the care of four junior officers similarly armed and expressly instructed to safeguard the agent regardless of the fate of the rest of the base.

There was a long time to wait. If an attack was coming, the Terrans were in no hurry to begin, and the unit monitoring the orbiting warforce reported no sign of unusual activity. Liam drank coffee and examined plans of the base and its surroundings to give himself orientation.

An hour before dawn the situation changed radically. A lone ship scarcely larger than a pinnace was observed to detach itself from the cluster of orbiting vessels and adopt a trajectory that would bring it to down in the vicinity of Base 22. At the same time a Terran cruiser carpeted the whole area with a close pattern of space-bombs, presumably to eliminate any pockets of resistance located outside the command-point itself. In the deep vaults of the base, the Benedict shield took most of the punishment, and the violence of the explosions was reduced to a dull background roar.

As the descending ship breached the stratosphere, one of Rakel's missile beds opened up with a period of rapid firing which seeded the space approach with a nest of self-targeting rockets. Such was the effectiveness of the shielding carried by the little ship that all these missiles failed. Soon the outside detectors began to pick up the thunder-song of the craft's retro engines torturing the night sky, while the flame of its burners could be seen lighting the heavy cloud layer from above.

"They aren't exactly keeping their approach a secret," commented Liam. "I think they deliberately contrive to descend like an angel of vengeance, you understand?"

The ship made planetfall a little away from one edge of Base 22, in an area where camera coverage was spoiled by the dome of the hill. They were thus unable to directly witness the emergence of the ghostly warriors from their vessel. A long period of anxious waiting followed; then an observation post at one edge of the base suddenly went out of communication. An immediate wave of activity swept through the control room, and Liam frowned as he noticed the tension rising with a rapidity apparently inappropriate to the circumstances.

Rakel was busy issuing instructions to a group of control personnel, so Liam seized a passing officer by the arm.

"What's going on?"

"They've attacked the base along a wide front, and they've already penetrated one of the storage bays."

"That's impossible, you understand? There's no way they could have crossed from the ship to the base without being seen. Nor could they have penetrated the Benedict field."

"Tell that to the ghosts," said the officer, shaking Liam's hand roughly from his shoulder. "By the time anyone saw them, they were already through."

If Liam needed confirmation, the evidence was appearing on the monitoring screens. Those showing peripheral views of the installation on the higher levels were already carrying scenes of a massacre in which a small group, in no way distinguishable from ordinary Terran commandos, except for the metallic sheen of their uniforms, were walking incredibly unharmed through a veritable storm of weaponfire, slaughtering defenders by the dozen. The impossibility of what he was seeing caught in Liam's throat. Considering the competence of the defense, not one of the attackers, no matter how perfect his body armor, had any right still to be alive.

After looking around for Rakel, who was nowhere to be seen, Liam rounded up his appointed bodyguard and indicated the battle scene.

"Take me up there. I have to see those ghosts for myself, you understand?"

Initially they were dubious, but finally decided that a safe observation point could be arranged. Liam followed them swiftly through the maze of subterranean passages, now loud with reverberating pulses of violent weaponfire and sickly-warm with acrid smoke. The invaders were penetrating even faster than his companions had estimated; the 'safe spot' to which he should have been conducted had already been overrun by the time they reached the higher levels. They halted prematurely in a long tunnel, the farther walls of which, blackened by an explosion, were crawling with fluorescent spots where some high-intensity radiation was engaged in searching out the luckless defenders in a side tunnel.

Suddenly a figure occupied the intersection directly before them. A radiation weapon flared and two of Liam's guides fell dead beside him. Liam had not seen the incident clearly because his two remaining bodyguards had dragged him into a shallow alcove out of the line of fire. Struggling to get a better view, Liam got one eye to the edge of the alcove, watched with bemused fascination as two armed apparitions stood briefly at the intersection, then turned and ran down a branch tunnel, firing as they went. Jon Rakel's description of them as ghosts was scarcely less than the truth. Human in form and movement, at first sight they could have been mistaken for Terran commandos clad in metallic foil rather than drab conventional uniforms. The crawling points of fluorescence at the end of the tunnel revealed, however, more startling truth—they were also partially transparent.

Then one of them turned in their direction and Liam was forcefully dragged back into the alcove only a split second before a heat-projector melted the girderwork reinforcing the corner, and showered him with flecks of burning paint. When the blast was not repeated, Liam risked a further view. By this time the phantom warriors had already moved into the side tunnel and were passing swiftly out of sight, but not before Liam had seen, against the absolute black of the soot-coated walls, that the ghosts actually glowed with a spectral light of their own.

Liam grasped his electron rifle, intending to follow, but his bodyguards restrained him.

"Don't risk it, Liam! You can learn nothing we don't already know—and you've a fair chance of getting killed in the attempt. Better we get you out now."

Grudgingly, Liam saw the sense of their argument. There was nothing he could now learn that the defenders of Sette had not already established; a repeat of his encounter with the ghost warriors was unlikely to add enough to his knowledge to make it commensurate with the risk. Regardless of how much he disliked the idea of leaving a fight before the finish, his own first duty was to report on what he had seen to the rest of the Hub, in order that others might devise a suitable defense.

The concussions which smote Liam and his companions as they began to run back through the tunnels were difficult to explain until Liam realized that a prime target for the ghostly commandos would have been the Benedict-field generator. Having disabled this, a further pattern of space-bombs directed from high orbit was able to pulverize the ground to such a depth that much damage resulted to the higher levels of the installation. This immediately raised concern about the safety of the flier which was Liam's route back to the waiting spacecraft. Liam was forced to abandon his intention of returning to the control center, and make directly for the vehicle bay instead.

The bay was in disorder, its vast roof widely cracked by the pounding of the gigantic high-penetration explosions taking place on the surface. Fortunately the flier was undamaged. Liam had a call put out for Jon Rakel to come and join him, but the message did not get through. After the destruction of the Benedict, the ghostly warriors had gone immediately down the lower levels, and were already attacking the control center itself. From the sound of explosions deep below, it was certain the arsenal was also under fire. With a heavy heart Liam realized that the burden of the decision of whether or not to surrender had already been lifted from Rakel's shoulders. Even if the commander still lived, the battle was irretrievably lost.

CHAPTER V

After seeing the Terran party clear of the ship, Dam sought out Soo Corda in her cabin. She listened sympathetically to his viewpoint, but gave him a quiet reprimand about his taking such a high-handed attitude with someone as important as the port marshal. Under the influence of her reasoned arguments, Dam began to see more clearly how his own attitude was beginning to color his judgment, leading him to defensive posture when only his pride was being threatened. He cursed his own naivete when she pointed out the certainty that all the ship's confidential records had been re-written on Castalia in anticipation of just such an examination.

Her powers of peaceful persuasion that night were greater than those exercised by Colonel Dimede on his return. When the Colonel re-opened the discussion there was a copy of a complaint from the port marshal in his hand.

"I know you felt justified, Dam. But these people have a different mentality; as much as being a fighting unit we're also—or supposed to be—ambassadors, showing the things we think best about Hub culture.''

"Which includes being polite to bullying snoopers?" asked Dam. "I thought the Hub planetary states were founded in the spirit of independence. That's a part of Hub culture too, you know.''

Dimede held up his hand. ''All right, Dam! Don't get yourself worked up! You know I can't discuss the politics of this with you. Rightly or wrongly, our orders are to place ourselves under Terran command—and that implies suffering gracefully all the provocation and indignities involved. It's all part of the job, and you can't kick at them without kicking me also.''

"In that case," said Dam, "I apologize and accept the reprimand.''

"Good. That fact will be recorded and the matter closed. But I was meaning to speak with you on another topic. Since we left Castalia you've been working too hard. You're screwing yourself up in a knot. We've some tricky missions ahead of us, and an officer already wound to breaking point is the last thing I need. We've a few days before our orders come through, so you're going to make planetfall and take some leave. Get into the bright spots and unwind.''

"With your permission, sir, I'd rather stay aboard.''

"A liberty pinnace will be ready within the hour. You'll be aboard it with the first landing party. That's an order, Dam.''

"Understood, sir. I'll be aboard.''

He found a room had already been booked for him at the Colonial Officers' Club. Most of the other residents were Hub men and like himself many of them were having their first experience of the mother planet. Yet he felt something in them he could not find in himself: an overwhelming excitement in visiting the planet where the human race began. The brochures in the hall listed extensive tours by strato-jet to the 'Cradle of Civilization,' the 'Birthplace of Man,' and similar places of historic and tourist interest. Dam was more interested in what the inhabitants of Terra had evolved into than what they had evolved from. He suspected he would find it difficult to justify the term 'progress' for the long years between genesis and the present supposed maturity.

On his way from the spaceport to the Club, he had already seen the rows upon rows of tall, grey apartment blocks of startling uniformity, whilst the guide had spoken enthusiastically about the philosophical and practical advantages of collectivized living communes. Dam, for whom places with more than two dwellings in line of sight were anathema, wondered what the suicide rate must be, and how all the pent-up frustrations and tensions could be released without blowing the social structure apart. He found at least part of his answer when he learned that there was compulsory conscription for Space Service; that took control of the younger elements just as soon as the school regime had released them.

He dined early at the Club, then, taking directions from some of his fellow residents, he went to explore the part of the city reputed to be dedicated to relaxation and entertainment. Only here, amid the crowds and the bright lights of the cafes, theaters, and amusement halls did any of the legendary magic of the Terran night begin to penetrate his jaundiced awareness. He was forced to admit that in terms of organized entertainment and sheer, brash enterprise, there was nothing in the Hub which could compare.

For a while he teamed up with a group of colonial officers he had met at the club, had a few drinks with them and was introduced to a few girls, but declined to go dancing. When the group finally broke up he was left alone in an open-air cafe seated beneath sprays of coloured lights and listening to the music played by a wandering musician whose beautiful stringed instrument tore at Dam's homesick soul with strange and evocative outworld melodies. He found himself sitting by an attractive girl who, though dressed in Terran fashions, had a faint accent which suggested her origin was nearer the galaxy's center.

Dam was not sure how they began talking, but he soon learned her name was Tez-ann, and that she had come originally from Gannen on an artistic venture that had failed. In order to make a living and to try to earn her passage back to Gannen, she had taken a job at the Outworld Cultural Centre. Such were the economics of her situation that after five years she was little nearer being able to return to her home planet than she had been when she started.

Tez-ann was easy to listen to and easy to talk to. Dam warmed to her almost naive honesty of approach. It seemed they were kindred spirits in their mutual dislike and mistrust of Terra and things Terran, and Dam found it encouraging to find another who so closely shared his own misgivings. While they drank and talked the wandering musician, apparently mistaking them for lovers, came to their table and played and sang them a soft and haunting love song that spoke of great desires and longing in other places and other times. Dam tipped him more than generously, and he and Tez-ann laughed at the mistake and began to pretend they were lovers and held hands and gazed into each other's eyes. Finally they began to explore the illuminated walks which led over the floodlit rooftops of the older part of the city, and she led him to some of the darker places where he could see more of the Terran night sky and its unbelievable paucity of stars.

When the night was half completed, and the cafes closed and music ceased, Tez-ann began to get more serious. She confided in Dam various indiscretions with a naive trust, insisted that he spend as much of his leave with her as he was able, and finally invited him back to her room at the Outworld Cultural Centre for the remainder of the night; adding that hers was not a living commune and was therefore strictly private. Reflecting that he was under Colonel Dimede's direct orders to relax and unwind, Dam could think of no more congenial way to obey orders. They set off together, arm in arm.

Tez-ann's 'room' proved to be quite a spacious and well furnished apartment, rather surprisingly so for someone professedly trying to save the return fare to Gannen. She answered his unasked question by explaining that the apartment went with the job and could not be exchanged for extra salary. From the literature and books around the apartment, Dam began to discover her involvement with a group critical of the ruling military junta, and he read interestedly through several mildly subversive pamphlets whilst she bathed and changed.

She came back scented and soft-eyed, clad in a

blue robe and bearing drinks in beautiful shallow glasses. The liqueur, she told him, was a speciality from Gannen and not generally available on Terra. Legend had it that love potions were once prepared from the same bled of herbs now used to enhance the flavour of the spirit. She was amusing and provocative, and they touched glasses and looked deep into each other's eyes as they sipped the drink. Dam found it unexpectedly heady, but a sudden suspicion came too late; when he stood he staggered and almost fell. Tez-ann's reaction was different: she hurled her glass away to shatter against the wall, her face a sudden mask of white anger.

"You bastards!" she snarled then crumpled unconscious to the floor.

Comprehending only that he had been drugged, Dam attempted to remain standing, but his sense of balance had been destroyed. He fell back across the couch. Then he too lost consciousness.

The next thing he knew was that he was staring into an intense light which rippled and moved strangely. At the same time he became aware that it was raining, that he was soaked to the skin, and was face-down in the open with his cheek in a puddle. His head throbbed and ached from what he found to be a heavy bruise over his right eye. The light resolved itself into a searchlight beam directed on him and reflecting from the surface of the shallow water in which he lay. The light itself was mounted on a hovertruck from which a number of uniformed men were descending.

"Don't make any sudden move, soldier! Just stand up nice and slow, with your hands on your head."

Dam did as he was told. As he stood, he stumbled on a dark mass which proved to be the body of a woman. The blue gown suggested immediately that it was Tez-ann, and he felt suddenly sick as he saw her injuries and realized her blood must have mingled freely with the water that soaked his clothing. Her head had been half shot away with a blaster.

"What . . . what happened?"

"We ask the questions, soldier. You do the answering," snarled one of his captors while another drew his arms behind his back and fastened them with a sharp wrist-noose that cut painfully into his flesh. Then he was dragged to the side of the hovertruck and made to stand there while Tez-ann's body was examined and the surrounding area carefully gone over with handlamps. Finally the body was removed to a second vehicle, and an officer approached Dam, holding out a blaster found in the water.

"Is this your weapon, soldier?"

"Could be," said Dam. With his hands tied behind him he had no means of verifying whether or not his own weapon was still in the pouch at his hip.

"Is it, or isn't it?" A savage blow across his face. Dam spit blood from a split cheek.

"If it is, I didn't use it. I swear!"

The officer motioned to his group. "Take him in and soften him up for interrogation. Get the lab to work on the wound and the weapon. I want this character and the girl positively identified, and I want all reports available by morning. If this colonial muck thinks it can come to Terra and start raising trouble, I'll be happy to set an example that'll dissuade him from trying again."

"But I didn't do anything," said Dam. "I can explain . . ."

Another blow across his face broke a tooth and so bruised his mouth that had he dared he could have spoken only with difficulty.

"Shut up, you stinking Hub excrement!" shouted the officer. "You'll do your explaining when we know the right questions to ask. I'm damn sick of you colonial trouble-makers. It's about time a few of you were taught a lesson. And I'm just the man to do it."

Still with no understanding of what was happening, Dam was pushed into the steel cell of the hover-truck closely followed by two armed guards. A long, uncomfortable time later the truck was finally backed against a ramp, and when the door was opened he was led directly into the grim reception room of a detention complex. Here Dam was ordered to empty his pockets and strip off his clothes. His uniform was taken away and a set of shapeless coverals was issued in its place. In changing, he noticed with some concern that his blaster had not been in his hip pouch. He made a brief factual statement, which was recorded without much interest, and was then passed through to the cells.

"Softening for interrogation," Dam found, was a euphemism for an hour of being pushed, punched and kicked by four guards who appeared to take a great delight in the slow and painful demolition of "Hub trash." Dam had never before realized that the Terrans harbored such a deep-seated resentment and hatred for Hub folk. It made it even more difficult for him to understand why Terra insisted on tithe-loan service from peoples she apparently mistrusted and despised.

The hour of punishment, which left scarcely a part of his anatomy unbloodied or unbruised, was terminated by the arrival of an officer in the corridor outside, who called the guards to a hasty conference. After that, his tormentors left him alone. Dam gathered that something had been discovered about his case which altered his status, but lack of apology or offer of release made it seem unlikely that the new factor was otherwise working in his favour. Suddenly the cell lights were extinguished, and he was left alone for many hours of pained and broken sleep. Return of the light heralded a tray of dull, uninteresting food, an opportunity for a cold wash, and a further hour of solitude before the door opened again to admit the scowling figure of Port Marshal Segger.

"Hmm!" Segger grunted to himself in substantial surprise. "I thought I might be seeing you again, Major. But this is quite a bit sooner than I expected."

CHAPTER VI

A power failure having made it impossible for the great doors of the vehicle bay to be opened automatically, they had to be winched open by hand. But knowledge of the importance of Liam's mission ensured no shortage of hands for the task, and many envious glances were cast at the vacant seat in the flier. It was an indication of the seriousness of Base 22's plight that the plans originally developed to ensure his escape had already failed. Liam waited as long as possible in the vain hope that Jon Rakel could join him, but there were dangers for everyone in keeping the bay doors open to the bombardment outside, and finally he slipped into the pilot's seat and began to study the controls.

Although he was a qualified pilot on his own planet, the control layout, indicators and conventions of the Sette-built flier were sufficiently different to make Liam doubtful about his ability to handle the craft safely. Nor could he still rely on transmitted information from Base 22. It was with something akin to controlled desperation that he finally tested the engine controls and taxied out on to what was left of the concrete pad outside. He was surprised to find that dawn had broken. The view of countryside he had seen through the night-scope on his arrival now resembled a bitter moonscape of overlapping craters and churned earth.

Though what remained was precariously insufficient the miracle was that any of the concrete pad had survived. Yet the continuing bombardment made it imperative for him to leave the spot without delay; he gunned the craft forward, felt it stagger sickeningly as it reached a crater's edge, then against all odds lift clear of the shattered ground and surge skywards after what must have been the shortest take-off ever recorded for a craft of its type. As it nosed towards the overcast, a series of massive explosions shook the entire terrain. It was Liam's private guess that the ghost commandos had blown Base 22's powerplant, thus completing the destruction of the command-point. He was so busy coaxing the controls of the unfamiliar flier that he did not have the chance to turn and see the results of the blast. By the time he had learned the automatic controls for direction and rate of climb he was well above the cloudbase and had lost any opportunity of witnessing the final ending of Sette's hopes for independence.

Liam's immediate problem was finding his way back to Wanderplas spaceport in the shortest possible time. If Terran Intelligence had learned that Jon Rakel had been inside Base 22 when it was destroyed, they would send in a full-scale occupation force before the resistance organizations could regroup under a new commander. That would put the spaceport very firmly out of Liam's reach. He estimated he might have only hours before escape from the planet became almost impossible. On his journey to Base 22 he had gained only a rough idea of heading, and since the craft had approached the base under automatic control, even his notion of distance could be widely adrift.

While the flier gained altitude he searched through the library of pre-set course programs, knowing that one of them must contain the instruction for returning the craft to the point from which it had come. Sensibly, from Jon Rakel's viewpoint, all the programs were labelled in code. Not having access to the cipher, nor time to experiment to see which might adopt approximately the right heading, Liam was forced to reject the whole series and to devise his own way of locating the spaceport. He found the communications set had coverage into the spacecraft navigation bands, and he called-up the *Starbucket* on its emergency channel. Euken Tor answered instantly.

"Euken, I'm in a flier about two thousand kilometres off, without maps or course reference. What can you do to guide me in?"

"I could flash-up the space beacon, but it would attract too much attention with us sitting out on the pads. The whole place is shaking with Terran ferry-craft moving in. It looks like the big push has already started."

"Your analysis is right. Sette is finished. It's our own survival we have to attend to now, you understand?"

"Right! I've been running direction-finding on your transmission, so I can give you a course heading, but I can't triangulate for distance. Set your heading for the figure I shall give you, and keep going until we can pick you up on the scanner. Once we can see you, we'll talk you in. When you can see the spaceport, land on the pads as close as possible. We'll be ready for instant take-off.''

''You're crazy if you think they'll let me bring a flier over the space pads.''

''They'll have too much on their minds trying to control the fire.''

''There's a fire on the spaceport?''

''Not yet, but there's a bowser of boro-flam in the quarantine area which should take about a quarter of the fuel complex with it if somebody was careless enough to lob a mortar through the pipe-hatch.''

''You don't get killed, you understand? We need people like you.''

Liam fed the directional data into the craft's computer, and was gratified to note that the new heading adopted by the flier was only marginally different from what he had derived by intuition. Then he started up the search scanners and began to watch for any atmospheric craft which might attempt an interception. The flier was armed, but only with chemically-fuelled target-seeking missiles, and would be no match for a fast atmospheric marauder armed with electron cannons.

As it happened, he did not need Euken's talk-down for final positioning. Visible from a great distance, broad vapor trails stretching high above the ground betrayed the location of the spaceport as a heavy concentration of Terran ferry-craft ran a continuing shuttle service to and from the fleetships in orbit. His final aid was a huge pall of smoke seeded with tongues of high-rising flame originating, no doubt, from where someone had been careless enough to lob a mortar into a bowser of boro-flam. It was a gratifying piece of sabotage, because virtually all the spaceport's stock of chemical propellants had also joined the conflagration.

Liam was actually in sight of the *Starbucket* before a trio of intercepting atmospheric craft swooped down out of the sky. They had been shielded against his search scanner and had remained unnoticed until it was too late for him to take evasive action. His first thoughts were that these were some of Jon Rakel's defense forces, and would recognize the flier as one of their own. However, they made a close pass of inspection and then wheeled rapidly, obviously coming in for an attack run. Liam was left with no maneuver he could use to secure his own escape, so he took the initiative and fired off a salvo of projectiles. The homing devices on the rockets were neatly cancelled out by the electronics on the attacking craft, and the missiles spun impotently off-course and twisted aimlessly to earth. Liam held the flier on its descent course, and prayed for a miracle which would permit him time to land before the wheeling interceptors closed on him.

The explosions which shocked the sky as the three attacking craft burst apart were themselves nearly strong enough to precipitate Liam's demise. Fortunately he managed to hold control and, by the purest chance, also to avoid the masses of debris with which the air seemed suddenly filled. The excellent gunnery which had destroyed his attackers in the last instants could only have come from the concealed turret implant on the *Starbucket*. While it had saved his life it had also blown the Z-ship's cover of quaint pacifism; the speed of their escape had now become more critical than ever.

He made a virtual crash-landing so close to the *Starbucket* that he had barely five metres to run to the hatch. Strong and anxious arms helped him through the opening. Nevertheless, the only thing which saved him from probably fatal cross-fire from the hand weapons of a group of Terran shipmen was the simple fact that nobody had been able to analyze the situation in the time available—they were using weaponfire as a warning rather than with intent to kill. There was still some apparent confusion as to whether the little tramp ship actually constituted any sort of threat. That uncertainty was suddenly dispelled when the decrepit-looking tramp made towards space.

It was conceivable that at the actual moment of the *Starbucket's* blast-off, the ships in orbit were unaware of the turmoil on the ground. This situation was swiftly rectified, however, because the little ship which rose between the lumbering ferry-craft was not only clearly identifiable by its outstanding drive capabilities, but was also prone to blasting out of space any other ship which too closely neared the path of its own trajectory. Equipped with a null-g counterforce of outstanding design, it was able to apply acceleration rates which would have crushed the crews of any lesser ships, and it speared towards space like a javelin hurled by some legendary god of war.

It did not have things entirely its own way, however. The carrier ships in low orbit passed their observations on to the ship-chain which policed the far approaches. By the time the *Starbucket* had clawed its way through the tenuous exosphere surrounding Sette, the ship-captain was already alert and waiting. Three Terran star-cruisers, each with the most formidable armaments available, covered the multiple projected escape paths, one of which the little ship should take if it was to attempt to pass. The automatic weaponry was calculated to reduce the chance of the tramp's escape to a statistical zero. To multiply their certainty, the Terrans further activated large fields of space-mines to cover the less-likely escape path prospects, and waited with instrumented expectancy for the fleeing craft either to be destroyed or to abort its escape attempt and to surrender.

One factor had been overlooked, however, and that was because their computers had never been programed to consider its possibility: despite having just climbed out of Sette's gravitational well, the little ship's frantic rate of acceleration had placed tachyon-space entry velocity within its grasp well before it encountered the deadly meshes of the ship-chain. Pausing only long enough to fire a salvo of self-guiding missiles at its would-be destroyers, the *Starbucket* leaped into tachyon space at a separation closer to planetary interference than Terran theorists had thought possible.

Suddenly become one with the strange particles of inverse space-time, the *Starbucket* fled at a velocity many times that of light, and despite the perfected instrumentation of the ship-chain her passage left no trace at all on the recorders. Liam Liam was on his way . . .

CHAPTER VII

The Port Marshall called for guards and had Dam transferred to an interview room. When they were alone again, he pulled a small recorder from his pocket and set it on the desk.

"Now, Major, you will please explain."

Dam related the events of the evening as accurately as he was able, concluding with his puzzlement about events in the lapse of time between his being drugged and waking beside the dead girl.

When he had finished, the port marshal shook his head.

"You're not as ingenious as I'd expected."

"I'm telling you the truth, Marshal."

"Let me tell you what I think is the truth—if you didn't kill the girl yourself, at least you know who did."

"This is mad!" said Dam. "I'd only just met her. I'd certainly no reason to harm her. And having only just arrived on Terra—as you yourself are able to confirm—I'm hardly likely to know who was responsible."

"Are you saying you didn't know Tez-ann was one of my agents?"

"No, I didn't know. I was gullible enough to think her genuine. But I suppose it explains the anti-establishment literature in her room."

"Precisely! It could well be that she was proving an embarrassment to your people, which is why you wished to be rid of her. I think you drugged her, then called in your friends. They killed her and arranged to leave your unconscious body alongside to make it appear you were innocent."

"I am innocent," said Dam. "And I don't have any friends on Terra."

"Such things can be arranged. We don't under-estimate Hub Intelligence here."

"I wouldn't know. I'm a space-soldier, not a secret agent."

"Yet you were briefed by Senator Anrouse only hours before your departure. Why else should some-one so close to Hub Intelligence bother to make a rendezvous with a junior officer? You see, Stormdragon, we know more about you than you think."

Bewildered and unhappy, Dam was returned to his cell, his only gain being that he had learned something he had not suspected—the existence of fierce espionage play between the Hub and the mother planet. Later he was taken to a different room and confronted by the officer who had been con-cerned with his arrest. The forbidding pose of the man was slightly tempered by the presence of one of Segger's aides whom Dam recognised from his visit to the *Starspite*. Dam sensed a schism between the regular military police and the security services as represented by the Port Marshal.

The officer put down the file of notes he had been reading, and looked at the aide before proceeding.

"Stormdragon, our investigations leave no room for doubt that the woman known as Tez-ann died as the result of weapon-fire by your hand. Radio-assay of the wound tissues gives an isotope balance consistent with that from a weapon of Castalian manufacture. Your own blaster, found at the scene, had been recently fired, and the fingerprints and the microtrace analyses of finger residues are yours and yours alone. Now what do you say?"

"I didn't kill her," said Dam. "I was drugged and unconscious at the time."

The officer turned over a few pages of the file.

"So you claimed. Wine and used glasses were found in the apartment, but no trace of the Gannen liqueur you described—and no drugs. In short, Stormdragon, your whole story is a pack of unsubstantiated lies. Normally I would beat a confession out of you, or you'd die in the process, thus saving us the expense of a trial. Unfortunately, however, there are security implications in this case, and this inhibits our customary thoroughness." He looked at the aide. "How do you want this one handled, Staff?"

"As quietly as possible. We don't want the security aspect made public because it would impair the effectiveness of similar agents still in the field. I think a swift military tribunal with a weak defence and a guaranteed conviction would best suit our purposes."

"Is this what the Terrans call justice?" asked Dam aghast. "I've done nothing."

"And you count for nothing," said the officer savagely. "Colonials are all the same—troublemakers to the core." He looked back to the aide. "Personally I think a trial is more than he deserves. I'd kick his liver out and then burn him with the rest of the offal. But if that's the way you want it, I'll have the papers prepared for the port marshal's office."

Colonel Dimede was later shown into the cell. His face was full of deep concern, and this made him look older and more frail than Dam remembered noticing before.

"Well, Dam, tell me about this mess you've got yourself into. It's not like you to get into a fight."

"Fight?" Dam was momentarily surprised, then realized the colonel was looking at the bruises and contusions on his face. "No fight, Colonel. These are just reflections of the judicial zeal of the military police. Here a colonial is considered guilty whether or not he's committed a crime."

"Did you commit a crime?"

Dam launched once again into an account of the events leading up to his present predicament. Dimede listened carefully and asked a few questions of his own.

"It's a wretched business, Dam. I'll get a message through to our Government Agents and ask them to intervene. If we can't get the charge retracted we might be able to force the trial venue to some world where at least you'll get a fair hearing. But don't build your hopes too high. You're not the first to whom something like this has happened, and our interventions have not always been successful.''

"I don't see," said Dam, "what anybody has to gain by putting me in this situation."

"Revenge?" asked Dimede. "You weren't exactly cooperative with the port marshal."

"Yet when he came here he seemed genuinely surprised to see me. Either the man's a remarkable actor, or else he wasn't involved."

"I'll send a message to Senator Anrouse. Perhaps we can get some government pressure behind this."

"That's another thing. The port marshal was interested in the senator. He thinks he has connections with Hub Intelligence."

Dimede shrugged. "Such matters are outside my province. But nobody would send an officer with your exceptional record on the simple errand of assassinating a prostitute—even if she was also a small-time security agent."

"Can it be arranged for Soo to conduct my defence?"

"We've already been forestalled there, Dam. We're invited to send an observer, but no more. We're appealing against it, but we don't have very much to use as a lever."

In spite of Dimede's attempted intercession, or perhaps because of it, Dam's appearance before a military tribunal was set for a mere three days later. In the interim the *Starspite* was ordered into space, leaving only Soo Corda behind to do what little she could for Dam. Each time she came to see him she appeared increasingly strained and harassed by the barriers of bureaucracy and probably conspiracy heaped before her, and no reply had been obtained

from either the Government Agents or from Castalia
itself.

The actual trial was, for Dam, an affair of purest
nightmare. During the night the prison doctor had
given him an injection of what was supposed to be a
tranquilizer. This had done nothing to calm Dam's
fears, but had induced a state of mental withdrawal
which destroyed his judgment of time and made
everything appear as though viewed through the
wrong end of a telescope. Even voices seemed mi-
nutely distant and difficult to relate to experience.

Bound in the straight-jacket of an unshakable
hypnotic state, Dam could only stand dumbly and let
his trial proceed. He burned to dispute the certainty
of the case offered by the prosecution, but the
sense-depriving fog which isolated his consciousness also inhibited his power to react. He found he
could respond with little more than a dull yes or no
when asked a direct question. Although deeply
within him a bright spark of awareness screamed for
expression, it was a sullen idiot who stood trial for
murder.

The whole day was clamped with an iron cast of
wrongness: time contracted to simulate an impossible degree of haste, and the defence acceded all the
important points to the prosecution. Dam watched it
all in numb horror.

After a while there was a break, and Dam was led
away while the tribunal deliberated. In less than
fifteen minutes—or was it seconds?—he was
brought back before the distant faces, waiting for the
president to enunciate, in crystal-clear yet micro-
scopic tones, the tribunal's findings.

"Major Dam Stormdragon . . . of the space territory of Castalia . . . found guilty on all counts . . . and hereby sentenced to death by military execution . . . within seven days from this time.''

"What's that?" asked Dam—at least he thought he did, but the dark barriers in his mind were closing fast, and probably his lips did not actually move. Faced now with an almost total inability to comprehend his environment, Dam staggered to the rail and tried desperately to collect his mazed senses. All he achieved was violent nausea; after which, and far too late, he felt very much improved.

Soo was waiting for him when he was returned to his cell. She was so angry that tears were streaming down her face. Her right to attend as an observer had been disputed until the trial was half over, the notes she had wished to present to the defence had been impounded, her micro-recorder had been confiscated, and her complaint that Dam had been drugged had led to her eviction from the hearing for being a 'colonial troublemaker'. To complete her despair, she had just been handed a letter from the Castalian Government Agents regretting they had lost the original correspondence, and requesting copies. The letter had, in any case, been delayed two days before delivery. She went away with the stated intention of getting very drunk, and that was the last Dam ever saw of her.

It was several days later that Colonel Dimede made planetfall and came to see him. Dam could see from the colonel's face that he was the bearer of no good news.

"Don't lose hope, Dam! The Castalian government have not yet replied, but there's still time. And

Soo has asked for a stay of execution pending an appeal. We're aiming to get the conviction declared void, and asking for a re-trial in some neutral setting. Unfortunately . . ."

"Unfortunately what?" asked Dam.

"The *Starspite's* been ordered into deep-space for patrol duty. We leave tonight. I'll have to take the whole ship's company, including Soo. So this whole matter will have to rest back in the hands of the Government Agents."

"Who've probably lost the correspondence again," said Dam despondently.

"Honestly, Dam, we've tried every mortal way we know."

"I know, Colonel—and thanks! The truth is, we're innocents abroad. We're outclassed by the intrigue and outmanoeuvered by the system. Could I ask you to ensure Tetri gets to know my side of the story?"

"I'll have Liaison send an officer to explain it all. And your record will also bear a full account. Regardless of what happens, this won't reflect less favourably on the name of Stormdragon."

As he watched the colonel's departure, Dam experienced a welling tide of loneliness. To the misfortune of his circumstance had been added a feeling of isolation from his own kind. He was incarcerated in a far place, among people for whom he felt no affinity or kinship, and he could see no way to right the wrongs which had been done to him. After reaching a level of despair beyond which he could progress no further, he began to treat the situation as he had finally treated all the other great crises of his life.

When the guards came to investigate the noise, they were surprised to find him laughing at having travelled thirty thousand light years to achieve so pointless an end.

CHAPTER VIII

On the sixth day Dam was transferred to Death Row. Here some human consideration was shown: he was allowed books and recorded music; and a sheet of unbreakable glass gave him a brief view of a succession of rooftops and a fragment of the street below. Dam spent the entire day with his forehead pressed against the glass, watching people pass in the street and catching occasional snatches of sound from the world outside. One scene that touched him with its irony was when a wandering musician—perhaps the same he had seen that night in the cafe with Tez-ann—came and played at the corner of the street. Dam strained his ears for the melody, but too little of the sound came through the glass.

To Dam's surprise, he managed to sleep most of the night without difficulty. It was only the disturbance of Terra's first-light that woke him with a churning stomach and a sick tension induced by the knowledge that this time of waking was to be his last.

There were still four hours before the execution was due to take place when he received an unexpected visitor. From a case a tall, pallid individual produced what Dam recognized as his own service record from the *Starspite*.

"I should introduce myself. The name is Abel. I'm Director of the Para-ion Technological Operations group."

"What's that to me?" Dam saw no reason even to feign politeness.

The man called Abel glanced at his watch. "I regret the late hour, but I've only recently received your records. I'm very impressed. The Hub service academies are doing an excellent job these days."

"Naturally! The Hub is where the fighting is," said Dam. "No alien ever got within ten kiloparsecs of Terra."

"Point taken! It's a record to be proud of."

"To me, it's irrelevant now. If you've something to say, get it over with. I don't intend spending my last hours discussing space academics with a Terran."

"An understandable viewpoint—and one I'd share in your circumstances. But paradoxically, it *was* your excellent academic record which brought me here. It'd be a pity for such talents to be wasted."

"Fiends in space?" Dam was aghast. "Go tell that to the port marshal. Do you think I'm here by choice?"

"I've already spoken with the marshal. That's how I come with a proposition."

"What sort of proposition?"

"We've an experimental commando scientific task-force on Terra. It's been so successful we need to expand it rapidly. Unfortunately, it's a difficult and dangerous job and we're having a hard time getting volunteers. But from somebody like yourself, with nothing to lose and something to gain, the difficulties and hazards might assume a different perspective.''

Dam tried to fold his breaking anger beneath an icy calm.

"Was this the reason I was framed for murder in the first place?"

Abel looked surprised. "I know nothing of your reasons for being here. I was unaware even of your existence until a few hours ago.''

"Accepting that for the moment," Dam said, "go on with what you were saying.''

"I'll make it immediately plain that what I'm offering is not life but merely an alternative to death. Should you accept, you'll be legally certified as having died. Your mind and your body then becomes our property, totally and irrevocably, to use, abuse, or dispose of as we see fit. Thus when we need to insist on iron discipline, we aren't limited by the usual considerations when it comes to enforcement.''

"And if I now spit in your face?" asked Dam.

"Then your execution will take place just as if this conversation had never existed.''

"What makes this commando unit so special?''

"Something known as para-ion technique— rather advanced physics, I'm afraid. By a process of electron stripping and ion pairing, it's possible to transliterate a man into a sentient gaseous plasma state. In this condition he can exist under conditions where no human could exist, survive substantial degrees of weaponfire without injury, be free from a number of physical limitations—and fight very effectively with a specific range of weapons.''

"Is this ionized state permanent?"

"No. Its maintenance needs a lot of power. It's therefore applied only for limited periods."

"Which is the difficult bit?"

"All of it. Both mentally and physically. Entry into ion state is equivalent to death, and emergence carries the trauma of re-birth. The only way you go through it is by iron discipline, both self-imposed and that imposed upon you. Especially in the training stages, the demands are frequently above the levels of voluntary acceptance. That's why we need apply extreme methods of coercion in order to achieve proficiency."

"I'd like a while to think it over," said Dam.

Abel glanced at his watch again. "I can give you an hour. But mark this well—the decision's irrevocable. Should you accept, it'll be no use regretting it later."

Dam returned to his window, where a view of ancient rooftops wet from the drizzle of a grey and cheerless morning seemed fully in keeping with his mood. From Abel's approach, he judged the man to be sincere: given that premise, it was necessary not to underestimate the intimations of hardship and danger. 'Not life, but an alternative to death' seemed an apt summation. His other route was to refuse Abel's offer and accept the finality of execution.

Finality—this was the key point. While he had life there was always the faint hope of escape. If he opted for death, that hope would be completely lost. He therefore decided to accept the opportunity for continued life, no matter how disagreeable, and work and plan for a means of escape and an eventual return to Castalia. To achieve this he resolved there were no risks he would not take nor suffering he could not endure: because having a goal and a burning ambition to achieve it, was the only mode of living that Dam knew.

When Abel returned, he needed only to look at the resolution on Dam's face to know which way the decision had gone. He took a solitary form from his case.

"What's that?" Dam asked.

"Let's call it the end of an identity. Sign this and you lose everything—name, possessions, human rights—the lot. It's the point of truth at which so many falter. In return for a signature, we issue a Certificate of Death. If it's any consolation, this is the last document you'll ever have to sign."

Dam read through the large contractural print, with the feeling that a large lump of cold lead was forming in his stomach. At the end he reached for the offered stylus and signed his name broadly and with a deliberate flourish. Abel reached into his case and produced, already written, a Death Certificate in the name of Dam Stormdragon, formerly a major in the Castalian Space Army.

"Think about it," said Abel conversationally. "Not many are privileged to see the document certifying their own demise."

"What happens now?"

"We wait until the time of execution is passed. Then you'll be transferred secretly to the para-ion training centre. Nervous?"

"A little."

"That's good. You'll need a healthy respect for what you're getting into."

"Tell me something. Knowing what you know,

yet faced with the same choice as you gave me, which way would you have decided?''

"I'm a coward,'' said Abel frankly. "I'd have preferred the long sleep to the anxious waking. I think you would too, if you'd thought it through fully. What sustains you is an idea that you can beat the system. It can't be done, but you won't take my word for it.''

"You're damn right I won't take your word!''

Abel shrugged. "We rely on it. While you've got hope, you'll be useful. It's when that spark dies that you make the wrong move—or no move at all—and I have to look for another candidate.''

"Don't you ever hate yourself for what you do?''

Abel did not answer. He had turned away and was arranging the papers in his case. All that Dam could see of his expression was the jutting of his lower lip.

For the period up to the scheduled time of the execution, events continued normally. Then a strange silence came over the corridors outside, as though all the prison guards had been withdrawn. Shortly there came to his cell a squad of armed men who were not of the prison staff and who had no sort of identification on their uniforms. Unlike the rest of the Terran military, these wore cushioned shoes and moved in almost perfect silence. Dam nicknamed them the 'silent brigade', and was careful to follow their unspoken instructions as rapidly as he was able. Having acquired the status of a non-person, he was in no doubt that these grim, quiet men had their own ways of dealing with reluctance.

He was transferred to a hovertruck in which to endure the long journey. Because there were no fittings, he lay on the floor and tried to relax; wondering to what sort of establishment he was being taken, and how realistic was Abel's prediction that the training stages involved demands beyond the level of voluntary acceptance. On his release from the vehicle, his first reaction was one of mild relief. He was in a camp built within a secure compound, but the informal grouping of the huts and modern buildings set between lawns and banks of shrubs gave no hint of a penal atmosphere. His silent guards marched him to a solitary interview room, and there left him handcuffed but unattended.

Soon, a female officer whose tags proclaimed the rank of major came in and sat behind the desk. She was attractive in the sense of having a good figure and rare, expressive features, but it was the sheer dominating power of her presence which whipped Dam's breath away. She had no paperwork of any kind, but appeared to be reviewing a mental record before she spoke. Her voice contained a fine edge of icy contempt.

"Technically, you're dead. That means you don't even have a name. The convention here is that we're all given call-names. Mine is Absolute, for reasons you'll learn to appreciate. What shall I call you?"

Dam opened his mouth to say something, then found he had nothing to say. The woman called Absolute smiled with some malicious vein of deep amusement.

"If my information's correct, you're here because of over-zealous attentions to a girl—scarcely hours after arriving on Terra. I think I shall call you Lover. The name promises to develop an interesting irony. Do you understand that . . . Lover?"

She was amusing herself at his expense. Even the

way she used the word carried a wealth of implications, none of which seemed remotely credible. With Abel's baleful predictions still fresh in his mind, he decided to adopt as low a profile as possible.

"Yes, Ma-am." he said quietly.

She slammed his cheek with a ruler with such force that it sounded like a pistol shot. Dam's eyes began to water, but he refused to give her the satisfaction of seeing him register pain.

"When addressing personnel, call-names only will be used. That's the first lesson you have to learn."

"Yes . . . Absolute."

"The training you're going to be given will be tougher than anything you've ever encountered. Physically, you can make it. Mentally, I'm going to have to toughen you considerably. I shall rather enjoy taking you through that. I shall even get a kick out of killing you if you don't make the grade. Do you understand me, Lover?"

Dam felt his old spirit returning. "I understand you're an absolute bitch, Absolute!"

He had expected her to strike him again, but instead she sat down and grinned broadly.

"That's better. I thought there must be a spark of life inside that colonial pig-skin. But actually you don't understand a damn thing. I'm talking about levels of obedience way above anything you've ever encountered. I'm talking about the kind of discipline which will make you respond when every atom in you is screaming rebellion. I'm talking about functioning in situations when your gut is tied in knots and the fear's so high it makes you vomit and go blind. I'm talking about being able to continue when your throat's raw with screaming, and death's by far the least of several grim alternatives. That's when you'll understand Absolute absolutely.''

CHAPTER IX

As he read the faces around the table, Liam knew the session would be difficult. Their expressions of hope and resolution were a cold comfort to him: the real message had not hit home.

Sinter Pauls, Liam's executive chief, motioned him into a chair which faced the examining semicircle.

"Liam, I think you know everyone here. We've been through your report on Sette most carefully. In the main we agree with your findings and your conclusions, and it amplifies and confirms several areas of rumour we'd hitherto been unable to pin down. It also provides a plausible explanation for the sudden collapse of the defences of Rigon in the later stages."

"But?" asked Liam Liam.

"But from the standpoint of known physics, what you saw on Sette is an utter impossibility. There's no scientific basis for these 'ghost' commandos. In fact, had the observations not been the result of your own personal experience, we couldn't have given the report much credence."

"Which is why Sette fell," said Liam patiently. "Because nobody would give credence to the rumours surrounding the last days of Rigon. Because you don't have a theory which fits, doesn't mean the phenomenon doesn't exist. It may just mean you are short on theories, you understand?"

Sinter Pauls shifted uncomfortably in his chair.

"Point taken, Liam! And this time we have moved. We've established a clearing house for any intelligence which appears relevant. And the Security Council has voted virtually unlimited funds for research as soon as we know what line the work should take. But in the absence of a suitable theory, we can't do much about developing a defence. Therefore we want you to set up an intelligence network which will give us something to get to work on."

Liam shook his head sadly. "Our enemy is time, you understand? Assuming they only bring their ghost squad to clear the hard core of a planetary defence, how many Hub worlds are you prepared to lose before you consider you've information enough? On your own admission, you don't even know where to start. I saw the proficiency of the Terrans. If I could obtain all the information you needed tomorrow, they would still have a ten year lead."

"Then what's your answer, Liam?"

"Total commitment on all levels by all Hub territories. Sabotage, espionage, infiltration of their base facility on Terra, and any form of armed intervention including outright war."

"There's no chance of that," said Sinter Pauls. "Very few Hub worlds are going to be prepared to show their hands at this stage, lest they go to the top of the Terran extermination list. In any case, I doubt the necessity to go to these lengths.''

''Sinter—if twelve ghosts could destroy Sette, how many more would they need to destroy the rest of the hub? About fifty is all, you understand?''

The caudal of Di was a trail of fragmented rocks and space detritus trapped between the gravitational fields of the planet Halcyon and its satellite Di. Such was the counterbalance of forces that these rocks were strung out as a trailing retinue which followed Di like a tail, hence the name caudal. The Terran ship-chain, if it bothered to observe the caudal at all, would have been unaware of the presence of a small addition to the fragments of the tail, so well was the *Starbucket* disguised for its latest role of simulating a lump of inert rock.

Inside the Z-ship, however, the situation was anything but inert. With virtually unlimited funds placed at his disposal, Liam had had the *Starbucket* extensively refitted, and its electronic surveillance equipment was now the most comprehensive and sensitive that Hub technology could provide. The Z-ship was currently operating sixteen data links with stations on Halcyon, using laser beam widths of only two microns diameter, theoretically indetectable to the Terran warforce in orbit around the stricken planet.

Like a spider, Liam Liam sat in the centre of his web, considering the constant stream of reports from his monitoring operators, and issuing fresh instructions with a rapidity which showed he had both a well-informed and an intuitive grasp of the situation.

Euken Tor, at his elbow, was assisting in maintaining the smooth flow of information and ensuring that every fragment of data was recorded in the computers for later analysis.

Even in the period of relative quiescence the Z-ship had continuously monitored the battle below and the exact functions of the ships in orbit. Now, as the little ship that Liam presumed to contain the ghost commandos moved out of orbit, every single piece of information it was possible to gain about it was meticulously collected, and the computer had begun to worry-away at the data. It deduced, surprisingly, the fact that the ship was remarkably heavy for its size and drive capabilities. This tallied with the information that it had been brought into Halcyon's orbit inside an immense mother-ship; presumably it was too specialized to have tachyon space capability of its own.

Watching its descent on his screens, Liam decided that the little ship's shields, impregnable thought they were, could not have accounted for more than a quarter of the unexplained weight. It was a reasonable supposition that whatever transformed its commandos into ghosts was immensely heavy and had a high power requirement.

Liam turned his attention then to the transmissions from Halcyon itself. As with Sette, the target area had been established in advance, but, forewarned, the Halcyon command had withdrawn the personnel from their fortification, leaving an automatic defence post peppered with Liam's special cameras and sensors and with the heart of its nuclear powerplant ready to run super-critical on Liam's signal.

By careful planning, Liam was this time fortunate

in obtaining a view of the actual touch-down of the 'ghost wagon'—as it was nicknamed—and this immediately confirmed the vessel's unprecedented weight. The whole area was under severe space-bombardment, which was playing havoc with Liam's sensors and communications, but luck stayed with him in the form of a long-range camera which stayed obediently trained on the ghost-wagon's main hatch.

When the phantom warriors began to appear they came not as a group but at precise intervals, as though each had to go through a specific preparatory sequence. As each ghost emerged, he ran straight to some pre-determined position and from Liam's point of view seemed to pass straight through the ship's own electronic shields without the slightest sign of difficulty. This same ease of penetration was also apparent when they came to pass without pause through the Benedict field around the Halcyon fortification.

The automatic defence system functioned well, even though it was ineffectual against its insubstantial attackers. Its function was not so much to deter the attack as to conceal the fact that the installation was unammed until the phantom warriors had actually penetrated into the fortified complex. In this respect its success was complete, and the commandos were well inside before they realized that the post was both unmanned and that they were under electronic observation. When the point became obvious, they cast about uncertainly, looking for reasons to explain such a strange circumstance. It was not long before they were engaged on a deliberate hunt for all of Liam's cameras, spectrometers and other equipment, which they destroyed as they went. However, by this time all the information the instruments could produce was already in the *Starbucket's* data banks, and the rapid savagery with which the ghosts had destroyed the prying electronic sensors made very little difference to the success of Liam's enterprise. There was only one experiment left to be performed, and with the memory of Jon Rakel firmly in his mind, Liam felt no compunction as he triggered the installation's nuclear powerplant into super-criticality.

The technicians on Halcyon had done their job well. When the powerplant blew it formed an inefficient bomb, but it was a bomb nonetheless. Through the long-range camera set on a distant hill, the watchers in the *Starbucket* saw the whole fortified installation rise with a slow, fragmenting majesty which soon obscured itself from view by producing an ascending cloud of smoke and dust. When the scene finally became clear again, the whole area appeared to have been levelled, and the ghost wagon, if it still existed, must have been deeply buried under tons of radioactive dust.

"That was dedicated to the memory of Sette, you understand?" said Liam, with only the slightest trace of satisfaction.

"You want out now?" asked Euken Tor.

"Not for a little. I want to see if they go looking for survivors."

"Survivors?" Eukon was astonished. "Down there?"

"I know it seems unlikely. But it will be significant if they even bother to look, you understand?"

By now they were monitoring the consternation

which the loss of the ghost-wagon had caused in the orbiting fleet, and were recording every ciphered message for later cryptographic analysis. The most immediate response was for the mother ship to disgorge a sister vessel to the one which had been lost. This sped out of orbit on a trajectory similar to that taken by the first ship, and it was deducible that a search for survivors was indeed about to take place. The descending ship was travelling completely without shields, and Euken looked at Liam enquiringly as if to ask permission to take it out of space with one of the major weapons with which the Z-ship was plentifully supplied. Liam Liam shook his head.

"It's more important that we see what they do when they make planetfall. If there actually are survivors, that fact alone could tell us much."

"Liam!" One of the technicians monitoring the Terran orbiting warforce was calling urgently for attention. "I think they've rumbled that the nature of the exercise must have been to transmit the data to a pickup in space. They're looking for us."

"Could they detect us in the caudal?"

"If they're dedicated enough to search each piece of rock separately, they'll find us."

"Then I think they'll soon achieve that degree of dedication. Euken, take us out of here."

"Noted and undestood, Skipper!"

Euken had their escape trajectory already planned and continuously updated by the computer. As the flare of their engines betrayed their presence to the seeking ship-chain, so the *Starbucket* swung up behind the cover of Di's tail and streaked for the protection of the mass of the satellite itself. Having gained this temporary protection, it turned abruptly and headed away for deep-space taking care to keep Di's bulk between itself and the ships now angrily breaking orbit for pursuit. It was a brilliant piece of manoeuvering, and though the surrounding space became brilliant with the explosions of exotic missiles, the *Starbucket* fled well within the narrowing cone of sanctuary provided by the rock-mass of the moon.

Aware of the implications, the Terrans put a hellburner down on Di and vapourized it virtually instantaneously. However, before the hellish plasma of the explosion could clear, the Z-ship had already achieved tachyon-space entry velocity; and with a ship full of priceless data and analyses about the ghostly commandos, they jumped straight into the relative safety of the strange fields of inverse space.

CHAPTER X

The system of call-names was a record of a malicious, destructive humour, primarily allocated by Absolute. Dam, who had never encountered such a tyrannical and vicious female, was both frightened and fascinated by the pattern of hatred and disdain revealed by her sadistic choices. He wondered how much of this was due to twists in her own personality, and how much was actually innate in the female psyche, to be revealed only in situations where, as with this female tormentress, their power over the condition of others was truly absolute.

It was on his first day that Dam met the character he knew only as Fiendish. The name seemed apt for the wild colonial figure with the shock of unkempt hair naturally curled in the tightest ringlets and eyes which appeared to stare constantly with a mad fascination. Absolute had left Dam in the interview room, and Fiendish, who appeared to be some sort of advanced trainee, had come to rescue him and guide him into the strange rigors of the routine.

Removing Dam's handcuffs, he offered Dam a

hand for shaking harder and more muscular than any the major had before encountered.

"The call-name's Fiendish. Welcome to the legion of the damned! Did she give you a call-name yet?"

"She called me Lover," said Dam, a little shamefacedly.

Fiendish whistled with surprise.

"That's not good! She's singled you out for some reason or another. And she's an absolute bitch at the best of times."

"Is she insane?" asked Dam.

Fiendish's face became speculative. "Let me give you some advice. Don't try and judge Absolute until you know her capabilities. When you've found out what they do here and how tough it is to do, you might finish with a different idea of Absolute. I know I did."

Accommodation was in separate rooms connected by a corridor, in a long, low building at one edge of the compound. The rooms were rather in the nature of cells, except that the doors were locked only at night. Each cell was furnished with a bed, chair, writing desk, wash-basin, locker, and an audio-visual teaching machine. Fiendish had a room near to that allocated to Dam, and giving the newcomer a short while to get his bearings, he came back and sat on the bed for a chat.

"Shut me up if you don't want to hear this," he said, "but there are three ways you can take what's coming to you here: you can fight it, you can suffer it, or you can go out and meet it. If you fight it, they'll kill you. If you suffer it, they'll let you suffer, but I doubt if you'll survive. It's easiest if you embrace it and try to conquer it. That's the way the system's designed—to eliminate the weak in mind and body. Only the strongest ever make the grade.''

"Whose side are you on?" asked Dam directly.

Fiendish took the question levelly. "My own, since you ask.''

"You're a colonial," said Dam. "You realize that a Terran commando force is likely to be used in engagements against the Hub territories—possibly even against your own world?''

"That's part of what I meant by strength of mind. There's no way you can beat the system. You either survive within its framework, or you don't survive. Unless you're dedicated to survival, you'd have been better advised to opt for execution in the first place, because this exercise includes some remarkably painful ways of dying.''

"So you advise collaboration?''

"The only thing that buoys me is the thought that one day I'm going to find a way to beat these bastards. And that's the day which will make all the rest worth while. But there's a point you've not yet thought of. They give you a teaching machine so you can brush up on the theory. Use it. You're going to get the chance to get an insight into a pretty rare brand of scientific warfare. If you ever do get back home again, think how useful that knowledge could be to some of the planets round the Hub.''

"Assuming there are any left," said Dam sourly. "But thanks for the viewpoint. I'll bear it in mind.''

Having thus given Dam something to think about, Fiendish seemed disinclined to talk further, and left. Dam examined the teaching machine and found the mathematical and technological material in the lecture magazines was of surprisingly high level, though well within the scope of the work he had already done. He found a stiff work program already laid out for him, and while part of his mind considered the implications of Fiendish's viewpoint, he began to work his way steadily through the first day's work-set. The lesson contained nothing he did not know, but the bias was interesting; and it was the promise of scientific revelations to come which began to dispose him seriously to consider the wild colonial's advice.

"Pain," said Absolute, in the first practical session, "has an evolutionary association with survival. The twin pressures of inheritance and later conditioning render it a factor to be instinctively avoided. For you, this is unfortunate. One of the features of the transition into and out of the para-ion state is that the process is acutely painful. Yet you must learn to make that transition without the slightest hesitation."

Stripped to the waist, and with his legs hobbled by iron bands and a short chain, Dam waited with apprehension. The other four newcomers, similarly restricted, stood quaking alongside. Dam could judge the extent of their fear from the sounds of their breathing.

"Which means," said Absolute, "that our primary sessions are concentrated on teaching you to unlearn your instinctive reactions to pain. We have a series of exercises designed to assist you in enduring pain levels within the range of normal human tolerance. To spur your dedication to the unlearning task, the guards have electrical goads which can range well beyond the tolerance threshold. Don't think we'll hesitate to use them."

Absolute was obviously enjoying her mastery, and she inspecter her new squad of trainees with scathing anticipation.

"You're over-rated, Half-man. I've seen starving rats in better shape. And Worm, better we bury you again—and soon. Creep, you've the texture and appeal of a plucked chicken. And I think the same sort of life expectancy. As for Neuter—God in Heaven! Do they expect me to make commandos out of this mess of festering sub-humanity? Compost would be easier. The process is already half begun."

She stopped when she came to Dam. The strength of his muscles rivalled the strength in his face, and the tan of Castalia's summers had barely faded to bronze.

"And of course, my Lover. There has to be a joker in every pack. You're not afraid of me yet, are you, Lover? Well, you've already called me an absolute bitch, so I'll promise not to disappoint you."

"If it makes you feel better," said Dam mildly.

For a moment their eyes clashed, and Dam prepared himself for a blow, but she conquered her feelings and turned to face them all.

"Something else I will mention. This is a tough induction, and a crucial one. Statistically, twenty percent of those starting the exercise don't make it to the end. So we'll simplify the issue for you. The one who makes the lowest grade on the exercises won't be alive by morning. Let that be an incentive to reach superlative heights."

"That's murder!" said Dam.

She rounded on him immediately. "Of course it

is, Lover! It's murder and sadism and brutality and every other stupid expletive your childish colonial mind can devise. What the hell else do you expect in a situation in which you've relinquished all human rights?''

"I know what happened to my claims on humanity." Dam knew he was sailing dangerously close to the wind. "What happened to yours?"

Momentarily, the anger flashed across her brow.

"I'm warning you, Lover. Don't try and take me on."

"What else are lovers for?"

"Right!" There was an angry decision in her voice. "You asked for this! Let's see what they make little boys out of on Castalia." She indicated a machine at the front of the lecture room. "Those two handles are electrical terminals. Grasp them."

Behind him, the guards with the electrical goads moved closer. Realizing that he had taken the exchange too far, Dam moved forward. The first touch of his hands gave no sensation at all, except that his hands became wetted with a kind of jelly with which the handles were coated. As his grip tightened, however, he received an electrical shock so violent that he was thrown backwards to the floor.

"Try again, Lover," said Absolute, and there was no mercy in her voice.

Despite his growing reluctance, Dam tried again. This time when he hit the floor he banged his head and partially stunned himself. He was a lot slower rising to his feet.

"Again!" said Absolute.

"It's impossible!" Dam was positive. "Nobody could stand that voluntarily."

"Nobody?" She walked up to the machine and grasped the terminals deliberately. Dam hobbled after her and watched her face, but apart from a slight hardening of her eyes she showed no reaction at all. Against the possibility that he was being tricked, he put out his hand to touch her wrist, and received a jolt which threw his arm high up into the air.

She released the terminals with a smile of triumph.

"Now do you begin to understand Absolute, Lover?"

Defeated in a way he could not have imagined, Dam nodded dumbly. The will-power he had to summon in order to lead himself back to the terminals and to conquer his leaping muscles was an achievement the level of which he would not previously have thought within his powers. Absolute watched his agony with a savage eye.

"That's good, Lover! You're learning," she said after a while.

Had Dam been forced to an admission, he must have said that the mainstay of his endurance was a grim determination not to be bested by Absolute. Without the psychological edge of this personal antagonism, all the others fared worse; and Worm, who was a native Terran, was driven to a state of frenzied hysteria by the conflict between the dreadful terminals in front and the excruciatingly painful goads of the guards at his back.

There were several exercises, each more painful than the last; and each Dam now met with the same savage attack and a determination to conquer which had enabled him to surmount the screaming messages of his nerves on the first machine. Absolute watched his progress with a critical eye, and if Dam faltered she renewed the spur by meeting the same challenge with iron-clad composure. Not to be out-done, Dam essayed the most painful test of all, and though bathed in copious sweat actually managed to laugh aloud while he did so.

At the end of the session Worm, whose skin had gone a peculiar grey, was taken away for disposal. Dam's three other companions had only conquered half the series and would have to return another day. Dam was singled-out by Absolute for special con-sideration.

"You did exceptionally well, Lover. But don't think I missed the fact that you were generating strength out of hatred."

"Did you also deduce whom I was hating?"

"Of course. It's a healthy sign. Something that will progress as our relationship develops. But it's a double-edged sword. I too have demons to con-quer."

She turned and borrowed an electrical goad from one of the guards, then holding it before her, she met his eyes squarely.

"Walk straight towards me, Lover."

"Onto that?" Dam could see from the control that she had turned the intensity of the goad to its highest.

"You can make it the whole way, if you really try."

Dam accepted the challenge and walked towards her, knowing that no matter what it cost him in pain, the price would be small compared with the cost of giving her the satisfaction of seeing him flinch away. With magnificent equanimity he walked straight on to the end of the goad. The burst of excruciating agony nearly robbed him of the surprise he felt as she let the goad slip backwards through her fingers so that he was pressed tightly against her when he stopped. Then she jammed the goad hard against him, and the rising crescendo of pain threw Dam into protective unconsciousness, and he collapsed like a sack at her feet.

CHAPTER XI

So fast had been the retreat of the Z-ship from the caudal of Di, that all attention to the signal monitoring had been forgotten in favour of crash flight priorities. The instruments, however, had been possessed with no such sense of urgency, and had continued to record the transmissions up to the point where the *Starbucket* had leaped into tachyon space. Without human knowledge or intervention, the last signals from Halcyon had been digitally encoded and fed directly into the ship's memory banks, from which they were only recovered much later when the miscellany of residual information was being 'cleaned-up' by the research teams in case any fragment of vital information had been overlooked.

Virtually beyond belief, the long-range camera viewing the scene on Halcyon showed that the sister vessel to the original ghost-wagon had indeed found survivors at the site of the blowup of the fortification, and that no less than four of the original twelve ghosts had been recovered before the recorded sequence came to its abrupt end. Liam Liam had the recording played many times before a rising suspicion caused him to study certain aspects more closely. Then he sat up suddenly as the image keyed a completely unexpected fragment of memory, which caused him to send the tapes for further processing to enhance the detail which had struck his interest. Finally satisfied with what he saw, he requisitioned the master copy, and ordered all other copies to be destroyed. With the master tape in his pocket, he left the research centre with a speculative look on his face.

Half an hour later found Liam in the central records department of Hub Intelligence, busily working his way through a reel of microfilm and occasionally punching the button which brought him a printed reproduction of what he saw on the viewing screen. Final comparisons made, he pocketed the printed copies and sauntered along to the briefing rooms where he was already overdue for a meeting.

This time he found the semicircle of faces more receptive than on the previous occasion. Sinter Pauls, sitting behind a desk burdened with files, greeted him cordially.

"You've really excelled yourself this time, Liam! The information you got from Halcyon is going to take months to digest."

"Months are becoming precious, you understand? Rigon, Zino, Ames' World, Sette, and now Halcyon. Who's going to be next?"

"That's what we were hoping you could tell us. Surely you've gained some idea of Terran advanced plans?"

"There's nothing I can tell you about something which doesn't exist."

"Explain that to me."

"The Terrans have no master plan. It's not that sort of campaign. They will merely attack anyone with whom they have a quarrel. Disagree with Terran colonial policy, and they'll claim to detect insurrection. They will attack and commit some atrocities with the intention of fermenting a genuine level of resistance. Having thus given substance to their insurrectionist claims, they then bring out their big guns and grind the defenders into dust. This achieved, they decimate the planetary population or sterilize the planet altogether, and look to pick a quarrel with the next."

Sinter Pauls shook his head doubtfully. "I know that's the superficial picture, but the deep logic still escapes me."

"That's because there is no deep logic. Terra is not attacking Hub territories because she needs territory in the Hub. She is attacking them because she does not relish the idea of collective opposition. She would prefer there were no populated Hub worlds rather than risk the rise of a second power which might challenge her galactic dominance. A dog in an interstellar manger."

"That doesn't make sense."

"Look at it this way. Terra has always been the home and the mother of the entire human race. Now, in all save military strength, she finds herself being outstripped by her colonial offspring. If the Hub worlds had ever formed an effective Federation, even Terra's military might could have been matched. Therefore she feels the need to divide and destroy the strength of the potential opposition. It's collective paranoia: the old bitch refusing to acknowledge her whelps' claim to maturity."

"Surely you oversimplify. There must be more to it than that?"

"What do you think she does with the worlds she's conquered? I'll tell you what she does not do. She does not populate them with her own over-crowded peoples, you understand?"

"I know it, but I don't understand it," said Sinter Pauls.

"She does not populate them, because that's how the colonies were formed in the first place. In two generations, Terrans become colonials, and the demands for independence start anew. Therefore she puts on the conquered worlds no more than a strict military garrison. It is this which tells me that the Hub policies of low profile and appeasement are irrelevant to the problem. It is not who we are or what we do but the fact that we exist which Terra cannot tolerate."

"I'll pass your comments on to the Security council, Liam. But I doubt if it'll have much influence on their policy. The worlds currently in favor with Terra won't want to rock the boat."

"It's illogical, you understand? Sheep or lamb, they'll all be eaten nonetheless. Whom she fights is a matter of indifference—it's the fighting itself which is important."

"Thanks for the viewpoint," said Sinter Pauls, obviously wishing to change the line of the discussion. "In the meantime, there are still authorized lines of action which remain the task of Hub Intelligence. Our research people have taken a preliminary look at the Halcyon information, and they think they can see how it's done. They estimate they can duplicate the process for inanimate objects within two years."

"When can they apply it to people?"

"No guesses yet."

"And produce defences against it?"

"Again no guesses, though something may be thrown up from other areas of research."

"Then I was not wrong when I estimated Terra had a ten year lead?"

"No."

"Sinter—do you realize how few of the Hub worlds will be left in ten years time? Too few to make a last-ditch stand against Terra even if the method can be developed. The time for collective action is now."

"While I may personally agree with your arguments, Liam, warmongering is no part of our mandate. We can advise, but there's no way we can change the policy."

"It is not enough, you understand?" Liam was searching the faces of his audience. "Senator Anrouse—you also sit on the Security Council. Can't you see the point I'm making?"

"I see it, Liam, but I know many who won't. You underestimate the terrifying responsibility placed on those called to make such decisions. Suppose you are wrong in your estimate of what motivates Terra? Have you really presented proof enough to justify all-out interplanetary war? Such arguments must swing most of the Hub territories or none at all: because if some go that route in isolation they are doomed to certain destruction. And the men who take the decision to commit them are themselves party to a form of genocide if they are wrong."

"Spoken like a politician! God willing, I shall write your epitaph: 'Here lies the Senator who took no decisions at all for the most impeccable of reasons'. Will it be easier for you to lose Castalia simply because Terran initiative took the decision out of your own hands?''

''That's unfair, Liam!'' Anrouse was growing angry. ''Despite your analysis, Terran activity in the Hub *could* be legitimately interpreted as the legal maintenance of the Terran Empire by countering insurgency. In which case, those territories who've kept their noses clean have absolutely nothing to fear.''

''If you believe that, you'll believe anything!'' Liam was undaunted. ''The extent of Halcyon's 'insurgency' was to quibble about tithe-loan conditions to supply thirty ships to Terra. The Halcyon Space Army only *had* twenty-three ships at its disposal, you understand? They kept their noses clean and got their arses shot off as a reward. If that's the wages of legitimacy, I'll remain a confirmed bastard.''

Later that evening, Senator Anrouse had an unexpected visitor. Liam Liam arrived at the door of the suite which the senator occupied when visiting from Castalia, and was immediately intercepted by Anrouse's aides. He was detained in a side room until the wishes of the senator had been ascertained. Anrouse agreed to see him immediately.

''Liam—why didn't you contact me first? You'd have saved yourself a deal of argument.''

''In my business it's unwise to announce your intentions in advance, you understand?''

''You're probably right.'' Anrouse closed the door and re-set the security screens. ''Now, to what do we owe the honour of this visit? You're surely not intending to follow-up our earlier exchanges?''

Liam smiled tiredly. "Hardly! Histrionics has its place, but without an audience it loses its effect. I wanted to show you this."

He took out the tape cartridge from his pocket and pushed it into the video player. Anrouse dimmed the lights and sat watching the screen intently until the sequence came to its abrupt end. Then he turned to Liam.

"The end of the Halcyon material, I presume. I've seen some of the earlier stuff already. What's particularly new about this bit?"

"Something the computers couldn't deduce. I missed it myself at first. Then a little bell started ringing . . ."

"I don't see . . ."

Liam re-wound the tape and set the image in motion again.

"I think you have not been too open with me, Senator. One of those ghosts I recognize, you understand?"

Anrouse let the sequence go to its end without speaking, then turned the player off and leafed gravely through the packet of photographs he had been handed.

"Was I right?" asked the Hub agent.

"There seem no use me denying it. You're a perceptive old devil, Liam."

"In my profession, I need to be."

"Knowing you, you didn't come here out of friendly interest. What do you want?"

"If you already had an agent in Terra's phantom warriors, why didn't you tell me before?"

Anrouse shook his head sadly. "For two main reasons. Firstly, no security system is absolutely secure. Therefore the fewer who knew about it, the better. Secondly, while it was possible to get that person among the ghosts, it has not been possible to get either him or any information out again. The project's surrounded by Terran hyper-security precautions, and in terms of intelligence returns, it's been an abortive exercise.''

"None the less, it could have very positive uses, you understand? I'm as aware as you that the Security Council's not going to be provoked into interplanetary hostilities. Nevertheless, I think your sympathies lie with mine. But there's a quieter battle already under way, and that's what brings me here tonight. I want to persuade you to become a subscriber to Liam's private war.''

CHAPTER XII

The sound began early one afternoon, continued all night, and reached full pitch the following morning. It had started as a dull, vibrant roar, which Dam initially had difficulty in identifying. As the day had grown dark, however, he had managed to trace the source. The sound came from a long grey building running parallel to the cell block, and containing square, unglazed apertures instead of windows. By standing on his bed, he was able to see through the air-vent that some sort of great furnace had been ignited. The noise was that of enormous jets of gas engaged in heating a large brick chamber which appeared to occupy much of the interior of the grey building.

As the night had progressed, the illumination from the apertures had grown sufficient to throw a rose-red glow across the intervening space and suffuse through the air-vent into his cell. By dawn the sound of the gas jets had risen to a shriek, and such was the level of the broadcast illumination that the fiery light glancing from the walls woke him with visions of hell-fire. Remembering that he now belonged to the

legions of the damned, he became fully apprehensive about the portent of the great furnace and what
its uses might be.

He was not left long in doubt. Absolute herself
came to collect him shortly after first-light.

"I'm advancing your training schedule, Lover.
We've just verified your academic level, and its
equivalent to three science doctorates at Terran
equivalent grade. That means we can skip most of
the preliminaries and take you straight into hard
para-ion theory. Your performance in the practical
sessions has been equally outstanding, so I'm going
to start you on actual ion experience right now."

"Now?" Dam made a sudden and unwelcome
connection between himself and the great furnace
which had disturbed his night.

"We've a training environment heated to twelve
hundred degrees Celsius—hot enough to make gold
run like water. I'm going to throw you in at the deep
end, Lover, because if ever I saw a natural survivor,
you're he. I don't know what motivates you colonial
bastards, but I intend to use it to my advantage."

There ought to have been a smart answer to that,
but nothing apposite occurred to Dam, so he merely
shrugged and followed Absolute apprehensively to
the grey building, whilst three guards fell in behind.
The air in the vestibule was suffocatingly hot, and
Dam began immediately to break out into a sweat,
wondering how Absolute apparently remained so
cool.

"Strip your clothes off," she commanded.

He looked for a changing room or even a curtain,
but there was no cover available.

"Here?"

''What's the matter, Lover? Have you never stood naked before a woman before?'' Her tone was scathing. ''Your reputation suggests otherwise.'' She took out an electron pistol from her belt and focused it down to a slim beam. ''I think you know what will amuse me if you don't co-operate.''

Dam began to strip, remembering the incident when she had coaxed him on to the end of the goad. Of the two devices, the slim beam produced the greater pain, and the deep burns took a long time to heal.

When he had finished, she looked him over mockingly, then reached into a cabinet and threw something to him which looked and felt like a bundle of soft, fine wire mesh.

''Dress in that.''

Dam inspected the mesh warily and found it woven into the form of a close-fitting suit of one-piece design made to encompass his whole body including his hands, head, and even his face. The entry aperture was small, and a considerable amount of manipulation was necessary before he was clad in the tight metallic 'skin'. An inbuilt resilience in the mesh made it hug his limbs and torso closely.

She now provided him with a heavy back-pack, the traps of which were of woven copper braid. Dam looked at the complex electronics in the pack, felt the harsh fit of the electrode straps around his torso, and for the first time began to feel genuinely afraid for his life. Absolute inspected him critically and made a few adjustments to the pack.

''Do you know what life is, Lover?''

''Is that a rhetorical question—or a proposition?''

''Neither.'' Despite herself, a glimmer of

amusement twitched the corners of her mouth. "Life is organization. Take all the compounds from which a human body is made and mix them together and all you've got is a revolting stew. But with the right organization of exactly the same components you have a thinking, living being. Factually, the organization is even more important than the materials from which the body is made. Preserve the organizational information, and you can transpose the being from one set of materials into another and back again."

"I'll take your word for it. Is this the basis of para-ion technique?"

"Exactly that. In a few moments I'm going to put you through the paraformer. There, every atom of your body will be stripped and paired with one of those of a host substance—in this case hydrogen. You, and everything inside your energy shell, will become quite literally transliterated into a gaseous plasma state. The back-pack is an energy modulator. It functions by producing the energy shell, and holding all the organizational information which makes you a being in such a way that your host molecules can't diffuse together and turn you into a homogeneous blob. Without the energy shell, of course, you would immediately diffuse away into the atmosphere altogether."

"I think I begin to detect the reason you have difficulty getting volunteers."

"Do you, Lover? The best is yet to come. There's a hydrogen-filled furnace ahead of you running at white heat. You have to go through the paraformer, walk through the furnace, and emerge through a second paraformer located at the far end. At least, that's the theory.''

''And the practice?''

''Para-ion transformation is a painful process. There's many can't face the idea of entering the second paraformer having experienced the first. For that reason the back-pack has a timing mechanism. You've five minutes to traverse the furnace. After that, the pack switches off. If that happens, better pray you have the luck to merely dissipate in the furnace environment.''

''And without luck?''

''You start a return to your normal state inside the furnace. It's quite a tidy system. Either way we don't have to dispose of any bodies. Just occasionally we have to sweep out a little dust.''

''Did you have to work hard to become such a callous bitch? Or was it a natural talent?''

''Quite natural, I assure you. And it's one of the least of my accomplishments, Lover. Now move!''

With the muzzle of the electron pistol she indicated he should enter a narrow tunnel. With considerable trepidation, Dam did as he was told. Ahead of him, at the far end of the tunnel, he could see a slope leading steeply upwards. Despite the hellish radiance of the furnace above and beyond, there was no doubting that the slope itself was glowing cherry red. The heat emanating from the environment he was being forced to enter was almost unendurable, and he felt his skin tighten as the sweat dried in the metal mesh in which he was clad.

He was actually standing in the paraformer before he realized it. Built into the tunnel's floor and ceiling, its presence was mainly manifested by its close complex of squared toroidal copper coils, beaded with moisture from the effect of internal cooling in the heated atmosphere. From this point it was possible to see the roof of the slope, where great transparent flames of hydrogen burned off in contact with the outside atmosphere. It was a vision of hellfire more real and squarely sordid than anything which had troubled ancient mystics.

He paused in the paraformer and looked back at Absolute wondering when his torment would increase. Her face was burnished rose-gold by the scattered radiance from behind him, and her eyes reflected back the bright flames in a way which gave the impression that they contained flames themselves. Momentarily he was transfixed by the image of her not as something mortal, but as a bright angel of Satan. There was something else he read in her face also, and that was a kind of passion he found no words to describe. He knew only that here was an image which would smoulder within him until the day he died.

She touched a control on the tunnel wall, and a transparent enclosure slid down from the ceiling to confine Dam in the para-former. Then Absolute came closer and spoke through a communicator system.

"Five minutes to get through the furnace, Lover. You might think of this as your baptism of fire. If you find your determination waning—just think of me."

"I promise you'll never be far from my thoughts," said Dam sincerely.

He was aware of a sharp drop in the air pressure as

large pumps started to draw the air from the enclosure. He was also struck by a curious deadening of the extraneous sound, and by a rushing in his ears as he began to fight for breath against the drastic withdrawal of life-supporting gas. Then the ion stripping and pairing process began: between the floor and the ceiling a great column of fluorescence closed around him, and he could literally feel the excited ions tearing at the flesh on his body, eroding him away. Every nerve fibre was exposed and separately corroded, and he was utterly consumed by a complete cocoon of pain which started at the outside of his being and worked its way remorselessly through his body into the very marrow of his bones.

Cursing, praying and screaming, he forced his mind to block-off and reject the messages his shattered nerves were trying to convey, and threw every atom of crumbling composure into the task of hurling wave after wave of dedicated hate through the impenetrable glass of the wall to the mocking goddess of exquisite torment who was enjoying his agonies from the safety of the tunnel outside. Then he became aware of a change that had taken place. He knew he was utterly destroyed; yet he knew this with a mind which still had sentience and therefore continued to exist. Reason told him he was dead; yet death brought no blessed sleep, only the anguish of a new awakening. It was an unholy metamorphosis, the substitution of a new creature for the one he had been: it was death and a re-birth, compounded of the traumas inherent in both. And he was through . . .

The glow discharge in the enclosure ceased, and the inner portion was raised away to allow him access to the red hot slope leading to the furnace beyond. At the same time the residual pain level died to nothing and was replaced by a curious euphoria and a sense of liberation. Knowing from Absolute's words that his entire being had been transliterated into elemental hydrogen, Dam took careful stock of his new form of existence.

His first reaction was to feel himself akin to a god. Although he had sufficient mass to give him orientation and traction, the weight of his old body had gone, and he felt his muscles were now capable of allowing him to jump fifty metres at a bound if he desired. His body was still visible, but now sufficiently transparent to enable him to see through it the details of the floor beneath. Incredibly, all of his muscle co-ordination and sensitivity of touch remained, yet the searing heat of the ascending slope produced no pain, nor did it burn his insubstantial flesh.

He looked back to see if Absolute was watching, but the darkness in the tunnel was too great to permit him to see her, and with a shrug of his shoulders he began to ascend the dreadful slope ahead. As he walked, he began to appreciate more fully the dangers of his predicament. Here he was, a human analogue composed of structured hydrogen, entering a furnace atmosphere of the same gas but in superheated form in which the molecules would be most violently in motion. The slightest malfunction of the equipment pack would most surely distribute him in the surrounding medium so thoroughly that even a sensitive spectrometer would have no way of determining that Dam Stormdragon had been intermixed with the furnace charge.

Apart from the pain of the transition, there had so

far been nothing to justify Absolute's remark about the waning of his determination. As he topped the slope and became engulfed in the turbulent white-hot gas of the furnace proper, however, the exercise began to take on graver aspects. The complete uniformity of the level of radiation destroyed any form of visual contrast, thus robbing him of the clues he needed for the judgment of distance and perspective. This, combined with the curiously 'thin' feeling of the hydrogen atmosphere and his own unnatural buoyancy produced a sense of isolation and sensory deprivation which coaxed him dangerously away from objectivity. The cold outside world of danger, worry and work seemed like the remnants of a bad dream; while his newly liberated consciousness stared straight into the vistas of a white eternity.

He caught himself in time, stumbled to a wall and determined its direction by touch alone, then forced himself to detect the clues which showed him change in angle of the floor, the ceiling, and finally a farther wall. Having discovered how to drag perspective out of his nearly featureless environment, he immediately encountered a snag. The furnace chamber was not the plain box he had imagined, but had a whole series of internal walls and apertures, a rapid examination of which soon showed that he was in a complex labyrinth, with his whole existence at stake if he failed to find the exit.

His initial reaction was very close to panic. In the first moments of para-ion experience, during which he had striven to come to terms with his situation, some finite amount of time had passed. How much there was no way of knowing, and it was conceivable that several minutes might have elapsed before his objectivity had returned. This left him a very short time indeed to solve the labyrinth puzzle and make his escape before the back-pack became inactive.

With swift decision he began to examine the incandescent walls, trying to economise on time by mentally discounting those inviting entrances which by deduction he thought must lead to blind passages. After several trials and turns he arrived at the point which logic had suggested to be the only viable route, to find himself defeated by the blank rigidity of yet another wall. With a growing sense of desperation, he retraced his steps, feeling that where logic had failed, only unbelievable chance could succeed in the time that remained.

Dam did not have much faith in chance, nor, now he came to consider the point, was it likely that this deadly labyrinth had been designed to separate good guessers from the bad. Absolute had appraised him as a natural survivor, and survival in these circumstances was to be earned only by a bloody-minded refusal to be killed. There had to be some way in which the unswervable intention to survive could positively affect his chances.

Then he saw what he had to do. The walls of the labyrinth were composed of thick, porous ceramic slabs. Seizing one, he shook it, and found it not be secured either at the top or the bottom, and light enough for him to be able to make it sway. Putting all his strength behind it, he managed to topple it, and its descent staggered the composure of several further walls. Judging his angles for maximum effect, he seized this advantage, and deliberately used wall against wall to bring the whole labyrinth to a scattered and leaning disorder. At one corner he broke through into a larger chamber beyond, and was immediately rewarded with the sight of the head of the slope leading down to the second paraformer. He ran the remaining distance with controlled desperation, hating to think that time might beat him where circumstance could not. As he entered the paraformer the enclosure dropped around him immediately, and it was only when the process had begun that he began to doubt his capacity to endure it.

The re-establishment of his old molecular identity was infinitely slower and more painful than had been the opposite transformation; added to which the return to an unpleasant mode of normality was a psychological imposition which his brain was extremely unwilling to accept. When Absolute finally raised the walls of the paraformer enclosure, Dam was curled in fetal position on the floor and sincerely wishing he was dead.

She kicked him with a metal-tipped shoe as a welcome back to the old reality, then helped him to his feet as he staggered back towards the vestibule.

"Not a bad performance, Lover! But you cut the timing a bit fine. You had less than nine seconds left when you reached the second paraformer."

"I stopped to chat with some friends on the way," said Dam, beginning to recover his equilibrium. "Tell me something, Absolute. Was there a true route through that labyrinth?"

"Usually there is—but for you there wasn't."

"Why not for me?"

"Because I've something very special planned for you, Lover. And I can't afford to back a loser. You've just proved to me that under ion-stress you can not only solve problems but can also see beyond and around the nature of the game. That's a valuable talent. But don't become complacent. I'm not judging you by ordinary standards. Hell, I've a long way to drag you yet!''

CHAPTER XIII

It was a measure of the desperation which drove the early colonists from Terra during the Great Exodus, that they preferred the planet called Lightning to their original home world. The planet was aptly named. A virtually continuous belt of storms gripped Lightning's atmosphere, her seas foamed with wind-blown spray, the thunderous division of her waves against the rocky fragments of the shores formed an ever-present background of noise, and her rainclouds were so thick as to endow the terrain almost perpetually with the shades of darkest dawn. The most frequent light in her sullen heavens was donated by the giant electrical discharges which ripped the air asunder in seemingly endless succession.

Less obvious were the advantages of living on such a world. Once the early settlers had forgotten their amazement and dismay and gathered sufficient courage to peer out of the caves into which they had run on making planetfall, they found themselves in possession of a territory so rich in easily-won minerals and organic resources that they were amply compensated for the loss of all but an occasional glimpse of the sun. Under the great rain-lashed granite faces of the landscape, they bred a tough and dour progeny, who built their massive houses in defiance of the storms and on a scale fitting to the terrain and the extent of their growing fortunes. With an innate sense of conservation they established an interstellar trade, exporting only the exotic sea-foods and plant products which were renewable resources. Their mineral wealth they kept exclusively for their own use, and in this respect they fared far better than any other of the Hub communities.

The covetous eyes of some less-favoured planetary neighbours, hungry for metals, had led early to the split of the Hub Federation, which had died in its infancy, leaving Terran colonial policy without effective opposition. The inhabitants of Lightning became introspectively defensive in everything but trade, and of all the Hub worlds it had become the one about which least was known and most was speculated.

Liam Liam's own first experience of Lightning had not endeared the place to him. The *Starbucket* made planetfall in the midst of an electrical storm the like of which he hoped never to experience again. The lead-dark sky poured down unbelievable torrents of rain, the thunder stung his ears, and the whiplash of the lightning pulses posed such a continual threat to life during the long run from the ship to the terminal building that the agent knew for a certainty that he had known safer situations when running before enemy guns.

Once in the terminal building, however, his equilibrium returned, although he was comforted to know that sixteen meters of solid rock stood between him and the giant electrical pulses which rocked the terrain outside. In the terminal itself, everything was massive and uncouth, while remaining functional and effective. Eschewing decoration of the mundane, the engineers of Lightning had built their installations with durability as a major premise and aesthetics a non-runner. They made extensive use of solid, unfettled castings where other societies would have settled for thin-section pressings, and having access to all the mineral and geothermal power they were ever likely to require, they consistently over-designed as an aid to strength. Their vehicles were so solidly constructed that each would probably last for several lifetimes.

This, indeed, was Liam's first experience of an amphibious subterranean railway. The canny engineers of the stormy world, accepting that the flooding of tunnels was inevitable, had designed their inter-city transport with this in mind. The ponderous, rusty, rack-and-pinion 'tank' which crawled through the uneven and flood-drowned caverns of the route made no concessions to the presence of storm-water nor had any concern for the sanctity of its occupants' ears. With his head aching from the noise, Liam emerged thankfully from the vehicle an hour and a half later, feeling that he had spent a considerable period of his life inside a water cistern. The journey had taken him a bare thirty kilometers, but subjectively he still counted this as one of the longest journeys of his space-journeying career.

He was now in Bama, the nearest thing to a capital city which Lightning possessed. Garside Raad, who headed planetary security, was waiting for Liam at the head of the long flight of metal steps which rose above the ringing cavern to which Liam had been delivered. The two men had been long acquainted, and Liam had acquired the greatest respect for Garside's insular yet fiercely practical approach to the maintenance of Hub independence. For his part, Garside was a firm believer in Liam's war.

From the method of Liam's introduction, Bama had first appeared to be an underground city, built not as a dome but as a confusing network of hewn corridors leading to illogically-placed establishments. It was only when they had penetrated to the upper levels that he began to understand that Bama was in fact built on the surface, but that all the interconnections between the various buildings were carried underground to avoid any dependence on the conditions of the prevailing storm. As he entered some of the buildings proper, he was also struck by the impressive majesty of what living could be like given virtually unlimited power and resources and a well-developed sense of practical values coupled with an innate hankering for sunlight.

Garside's offices were in a bluff tower whose massive integrity was unshaken by the storm which blazed beyond the triple-glazed windows. Here Liam was handed the actual documents with which Terra announced her findings of insurrection on Lightning, and her intention of countering with armed intervention. He read the papers carefully, then laid them back on the desk and looked up to meet Garside Raad's gaze.

"Don't say it. I...

..........., Liam! I know you told us so. The question is what's the next move."

"How much government backing have you got?"

"They've given me absolute control. That's why I

asked you here. We've seen what happened to the others without the benefit of Liam's war. Well, you've proved your point right down the line. This time we want to try it your way. We're meeting the President for supper, but I wanted to have this discussion first.''

''I can't promise you miracles, you understand? My overall plans concern the salvation of the Hub, not individual worlds. It's conceivable we may lose Lightning before we can stop Terra.''

''That's a prospect we've already faced. History tells us we're already lost. If you can salvage or save us anything at all, we'll be that much ahead of the game. We're completely at your disposal.''

''Those are the only conditions I can accept. Normally, the course of the battle is carefully engineered by Terran architects. This time there must be a different sequence, as defined by the scribble-pad of Liam Liam, you understand? There is something the Terrans will be bringing with them which it is absolutely vital we acquire. It must be acquired even if we lose Lightning in the process. Now I suggest we start discussion of the details before we meet the President.''

The Terran campaign against Lightning ran into trouble from the start. Unexpectedly, their menacing orbital fleet around the planet came under fire, not from ground-based resources but from sophisticated and unidentified ships which leaped suddenly out of tachyon space, released series after series of punishing missiles, and leaped back out of normal space before answering fire could be made effective. There was even a suspicion that some of the missiles had a tachyon-space capability of their own, and had been pre-directed at the ship-chain from a safe position many parsecs away.

Although the Terran forces learned to live with the situation, their losses were such as to make it necessary to foreshorten the whole campaign and thus remove the necessity to maintain a vulnerable fleet in orbit around the planet. They deposed the government of Lightning, drafted in a corps of military administrators, carried out severe punitive raids on any manifest pockets of resistance, and generally satisfied themselves that whoever was attacking the ship-chain was doing so with resources beyond the reach of the indigenous opposition which still functioned on the planet. In the meantime their space-borne losses tripled.

The Terrans had identified two substantial pockets of resistance on Lightning, both occupying former-city sites well suited for defence and virtually proof against space-bombing by the sheer strength of the rock-mass under which their installations and supply-lines were concealed. An attempt to over-run these areas with conventional space-marine forces was met by a conspiracy of terrifying weather and good old defence tactics, and turned into a major disaster for the Terran force. That same evening they also lost their orbiting flagship and an unnerving percentage of their local high-command.

The Terran Reserve Commander picked up the reins immediately, found the morale of his force shatteringly low, and determined to end the whole campaign as swiftly as possible. Thus, under cover of one of the most drastic space bombardments ever devised, the little ship of Para-Ion Command left the

womb of its mother ship and made its way venge-
fully down to the planet's surface. Soon its ghostly
company had entered one of the main areas of resistance, and was exploring a vertible catacomb of
underground defences, encountering very little opposition save for mines and booby-traps set in abun-
dance, which the intruders took in their stride. Of the
supposed defenders there was no sign at all.

Suspecting the sort of trap they had encountered
on Halcyon, the officer commanding the phantom
warriors ordered an immediate withdrawal, but he
was too late. Whereas the explosion on Halcyon had
been the calculated blow-up of a nuclear power
plant, the blast which opened up the ancient and
unwilling mountains of Lightning was an ultra-
sophisticated fusion weapon. This time there seemed
little doubt of the ion warriors' destruction.

Nor was this the end of the period's dismay. While
the orbiting fleet was examining the evidence of the
catastrophic blast which had shattered their secret
weapon, a new alert was sounded. Like a hundred
tiny piranha fish, single-man lifecraft of a size individually too small to trigger the long-range alarms,
had risen unnoticed from the planet's surface and
were converging on the mother ship, which, with her
screens inactive, was attempting to launch the sister
to the ship lost in the surface blast.

Terran fury turned to dismay when it was found
that there was no way in which they could turn their
arms on the miniscule fleet of intruders without a
very real chance of damaging or destroying their
own unshielded mother ship. The Reserve Commander was in an agony of indecision, not knowing
whether to order the destruction of everything in that

area regardless—in which case he lost not only the mother ship but the second ghost-wagon and its ion-crew as well—or whether to take on the new-comers with more conventional space-commando tactics. He chose the latter course, and played right into Liam Liam's hands.

In order to launch the commando pinnaces, it was necessary for the warships to lift their own shields. Scarcely had this been done when a number of un-identified spacecraft leaped out of tachyon space in incredibly close proximity, and sitting undisturbed behind their own screens, calmly started picking the exposed Terran warships out of space. There fol-lowed a period of chaos, in which the Terran carrier ships hastily jettisoned their own commando forces and strove to ensure their own survival. So precise was Liam's anticipation of the event that a quarter of the orbital warforce had been destroyed before the remaining Terran vessels had secured themselves sufficiently to begin aggressive action. At this point the unidentified attackers withdrew. When the Ter-rans finally came to count the cost of the battle, they were forced to include one mother ship and its back-up 'ghost-wagon' daringly hijacked from the centre of the fleet.

That night there was rejoicing on Lightning, but it was a revelry overshadowed with the knowledge that Terra's final retribution would be massive and terri-ble. Nevertheless, Liam Liam's signal from the *Starbucket* with the news that the mission had been a complete success was a promise for the future. Perhaps Lightning itself would not escape despoila-tion at Terra's hands, and Liam's private space army, though daily growing stronger by anonymous donations of money and ships, was yet but a gnat in the jungle of Terra's might; but here at last was a shaft of hope which could penetrate down through even Lightning's brooding skies, and its touch was as welcome as that of their own shy sun.

CHAPTER XIV

Only later did Dam discover from the mad-eyed Fiendish that his own recent exposure to the para-ion furnace had actually taken him through three grades of the training exercise simultaneously. He was now separated from his initial training squad and set to work with a group of more advanced trainees, of which Fiendish was one. Amongst these, the attitude to training was entirely different, because the selective murder of those physically or psychologically unable to respond to the effort had already reduced the survivors to those of a like type—fit, tough, and educated men, mainly ex-colonial officers, grimly united in their intention of surviving whatever they were forced to endure and to watch constantly for the opportunity to escape.

This advanced group was now engaged in regular training in gas and natural environments and in the use of various radiation weapons while in para-ion state. Dam was particularly interested in 'open atmosphere' work, in which, after having been given an ion-identity in the paraformer, the training took place primarily in the open fields of the establishment, where the potential for escape was obvious. It was here, however, that Dam also began to appreciate how carefully woven were the traps which kept them in bondage.

Each time they adopted an ion-identity, a present time limit was programed into their information modulator packs; and before the expiration of the set time it was necessary for each to return through the paraformer for the re-establishment of normal molecular identity. Failure to meet this deadline meant complete destruction as the modulator pack ceased to maintain the energy shell which maintained them in ion-state. There was a dramatic example of this when they were working in a para-phosphorus identity out in the damp grass of the long field. One of their number, a Terran call-named Spiteful, suddenly burst into a phosphorus fire that consumed him utterly. The agony of his cries as he partially reverted to his normal identity at the same time as burning away was a shocking reminder that they all continued their existence balanced on the razor's edge of sufferance.

Absolute had watched the man's agonized death with an equanimity which convinced Dam that she had actually contrived to achieve the fellow's death. Certainly she showed no reaction other than a slightly critical contempt. Dam shot a look at Fiendish, and was surprised to note, after the initial shock had died away, that his wild expression relaxed to one of questing speculation rather than anger or horror or any of the emotions that might have been expected. For his part, Dam could scarcely wait for the opportunity to regain normal molecular identity. He felt the need to be violently sick.

From this and similar incidents, many things about the exercise were becoming clear to Dam, particularly the point of the earlier exercises designed to encourage deliberate acceptance of pain. The para-ion transition was an experience seemingly suited to stimulate all the nerves of the body, and repeated exposure to its torment began to build up a conditioned resistance to the ordeal which at times became insurmountable by will-power. Even the most practised would occasionally arrive at a point of hysteria where they were literally unable to force their limbs to take them into the paraformer. So high were the penalties to be paid for delay in achieving the transition within the set time that the group would aid each other by main force if necessary, and this had bred a mutual dependence and comradery which grew stronger the more critical the training conditions became.

It was after the phosphorus burn-up, with the nausea flooding inside him, that Dam found his limbs would not respond to his command. Fiendish was the one who thrust him forcibly into the paraformer chamber, and it was Fiendish who caught his retching shoulders when the transition was over and guided him away from Absolute's malevolent attention.

"Stick it out, Lover! Sometimes it happens."

Dam shook his head sickly. "I guess it was that phosphorus burn which touched me off."

"I know what you mean—but there's another way of viewing things like that. Statistically it could be working in our favour."

"How do you make that out?"

"The initial intake here is mainly of colonials,

with a very few Terrans. Because of the continual wastage during training, the top percentage who make the course right to the end are almost exclusively colonials.''

''I hadn't realized that.''

''There's an even more curious fact. Talking percentages, not only is the indigenous Terran intake lower, but their loss-rate is significantly higher. Sometimes I'd almost swear that bitch Absolute was killing them off deliberately.''

''That doesn't make sense, Fiendish.''

''I know it.'' Fiendish's wild stare became madder than ever. ''But one day the organization's going to make one little slip—and on that day they're going to find a very mean and bitter colonial army corps with para-ion capability sitting right in their midst.''

''You think the organization's likely to make a slip?''

''Things are changing. Rumour has it they've had a lot of losses of para-ion people in the field. That's why the training schedule here has been accelerated. Also there's a new technique on its way. Human nature being what it is, someone somewhere down the line has to make a mistake once the routine is broken. Keep watching for it, Lover. I've a feeling that time is on our side.''

The following day they were introduced to the concept of 'transience' in para-ion work; and the method of its presentation was notable for its dramatic effect and for providing an excuse for Absolute to work out some of the strange twists in her character. As usual when she was feeling vicious she chose to concentrate on Dam. For a reason which had not been explained, Dam had been clad that morning not in his usual fine mesh suit but in one coarser and stiffer, which hampered and slowed his movements considerably. Perversely, Absolute had chosen complex exercises involving climbing and leaping between high concrete towers for the morning's work, laying stress on the advantages of the para-ion state to give reduced weight while maintaining normal muscle power.

Clad in his ungainly suit, Dam performed badly right from the start. His performance was not improved by Absolute's critical cursing and bitching at his heels. Physically almost exhausted by the unfair struggle and irked close to the end of his endurance, Dam was finally led to protest. She rounded on him instantly, a look of challenging and amused incredulity on her face.

"I hope you're not complaining, Lover—after all I've done for you!"

"So it amuses you to play games? How does that assist my training in para-ion technique?"

"More than you suspect. You're my star pupil— very well, let's see you burning brightly. You'll repeat the last exercise, but in half the original time."

"You're mad! It can't be done. Especially not in this suit."

"Nonetheless, you'll do it." Her eyes were very dangerous. "Otherwise I may have to transfer my attentions elsewhere, my Lover." She looked round, seized an auto-carbine from one of the guards, and pointed it at Dam menacingly. "Now move!"

Knowing it was hopeless before he even started, Dam made an attempt. He stood no chance at all. In a leap between two concrete towers he could not gain sufficient momentum to carry him over the gap. He plunged down between the towers in a fall which would have killed him had he not been in a para-ion identity, and even in his ionic condition he was severely dazed and shaken.

As he collected himself he heard a sort of snarl and turned to find Absolute moving towards him, carbine in hand and a hideous determination on her face. Dam had just opened his mouth to say something, when she fired the carbine point-blank at his chest. Jaw still dropped, the amazed Dam heard the bullet ricochet from the base of the practice tower behind him, and knew that it must have passed right through his body although he felt no pain or any effect of injury.

Eyes narrowed with the kind of passion Dam had seen on her face at the time of his first entry into a paraformer, Absolute switched the carbine on to automatic fire and discharged the whole magazine at him in a pattern which should have cut him into pieces. Not until the last bullet had left the barrel did she rest the weapon and allow her face to relax into a triumphant smile.

"That did me a power of good, Lover! What did it do for you?"

"Hell!" Dam had turned to examine the base of the practice tower, where the material had been shattered and fragmented by the repeated impact of the high-velocity projectiles. For himself he felt nothing out of the ordinary, yet he had to accept the fact that the contents of the entire magazine had passed through his body.

"Transience," said Absolute. "Phenomena

above a certain threshold velocity can pass through a body in para-ion state without disturbing the integrity of the information contained in the energy shell. Thus you should be able to survive weapon-fire or a near explosion. It's the slower-moving debris which will present more of a danger. And even there you still have an advantage—albeit a painful one—inasmuch as providing that the energy shell remains intact it can withstand considerable distortion before it fails to maintain the life analogue contained with in.''

"Explain that to me," said Dam.

"Briefly, you could be crushed alive to an incredible degree and still stand a good chance of survival. Of course, your analogue body would feel every normal indication of the injury until the original shell configuration had been restored, but that's a small price to pay for a kind of lesser immortality.''

"Or the price of the privilege of dying more than once?''

She looked into his face, and her eyes said something deep but indefinable, then she turned and walked away, motioning the rest of the group back to form a wide arc. Realizing that another demonstration was about to take place, Dam remained where he was, still trying to come to terms with the idea of having been riddled with bullets and yet having survived. He had no wish to participate further in any of her new revelations about the potential of the para-ion state.

It was only when something detonated somewhere near the top of one of the practice towers that Dam realized he was already a participant in the next demonstration. Summoning the whole of his para-ion capability, he attempted to leap clear, but the tower fragmented into large, precalculated pieces which fell on and around him, pinning him to the ground and crushing him mercilessly. As Absolute had predicted, his ion-analogue body felt every phase of the injury just as his natural body would have done, up to the point where merciful uncon-sciousness intervened to block his awareness of the pain.

Yet when he awoke there was no pain, only the memory and the fear of it. His comrades, with bars and bare hands, had shifted back the debris of the tower, and now he lay in a clear space believing himself to be dead and wondering how in death he could still summon a living consciousness. Then Absolute came over and peered down at him with no trace whatever of concern.

"Get on your feet, Lover! We don't give rest days here. You've just finished your training course right up to the actual combat stage—and in about a tenth of the normal time. I said I wasn't judging you by ordinary standards. So tomorrow I'm going to start you on something new and experimental."

Dam, who had supposed his lack of further pain to be due to nervous injury or a pain-killing injection, was overcome by an immense surge of emotion which manifested itself in a burst of blind anger as he found he was still functioning and able to move. More from her expression than from her movements, he read Absolute's next intention, and as her foot travelled towards his ribs he twisted with the speed of a cobra, seized her ankle, and threw her off-balance. Instead of kicking him, she fell on top of him. He could feel her shaking spasmodically as she lay, and wondered what unimaginable spasm of anger he had aroused. But when he rolled her over she was laughing.

CHAPTER XV

In the quiet room, Liam Liam read the report with eyes which became increasingly grave. Sinter Pauls and the others maintained a discreet silence until he was finished. Finally the agent laid the document back on the curved table and turned to face the assembly.

"That was inevitable, you understand?"

"Was it, Liam?" asked Sinter Pauls. "You were given leave to carry out an intelligence mission on Lightning—and don't let's be mistaken, you did a brilliant job. But the scale of your exercise leaves the rest of the Hub worlds open to a charge of armed intervention. Decades of carefully maintained neutrality have been jeopardized, and Terra now has a very good case for punitive reprisals against almost any world in the Hub. Are you deliberately trying to drag us into war?"

"You're playing with words," said Liam scornfully. "It's an idiocy of politicans that they can't distinguish between words and deeds. Terra was already attacking where and when she chose. All that's changed is that she doesn't now need voice such elaborate justification for doing what she intended to do anyway."

"Nonetheless," Sinter Paul's voice was serious, "the Terran General Ultimatum has shaken the Hub Council to the core. Suddenly each world sees itself as a potential battlefield."

"Which is nothing but the reality I've been preaching for years. Surely here's the impetus we need to make a joint effort to halt Terra. Against a united Hub, there's no way the mother-planet could win."

"The Council's aware of your advocacy of interstellar war, but they don't subscribe to your ideas. In fact they take the reverse view. In their opinion, your activities are endangering interstellar peace. Frankly, what has become known as Liam's war must cease."

"Cease?" Liam rose to his feet angrily. "That's out of the question, you understand?"

"That's an order, Liam."

"And if I refuse?"

"Then I've no alternative but to dismiss the Service. Sorry, ... dismiss you from , ..., Liam, but that's the way it has to be."

"Sinter—you're incredible! Surely you don't subscribe to this insanity?"

"Unfortunately my own feelings are irrelevant to the issue. I have a directive to enforce. Either you terminate Liam's war against Terra, or you cease to be a member of Hub Intelligence. Black or white— no shades of grey. How do you answer?"

Attempting to control the storm rising within him, Liam, hands clenched the desk edge, longing to pound his anger into the wood, but remaining motionless with only the whiteness of the knuckles to betray the tension.

"Sinter, you know what my answer must be. I've already acquired certain resources donated by some who do not have their heads buried in the sand. It would be easier with your help, but even without it Liam's war must continue. There is no alternative, you understand?"

"I will give you ten seconds to change your mind."

"Sinter, you know me!"

"Yes, I know you, Liam. That's why I had your discharge papers already prepared. Your dismissal takes immediate effect, and the Council will be so informed. Now sit down and let's get on with the rest of the business."

"What?"

"I said sit down, Liam! As an ex-member of Hub Intelligence, you've no right to be still on the premises. I should hate to notice you hanging around. Senator Anrouse, I think you had a point to raise."

"Yes indeed!" Anrouse rose to his feet. "The Castalian Space Army Command has been checking its inventory, and some gross accounting errors have come to light. Briefly, we're about to write-off from the books nine major warcraft."

"Nine? That sounds rather careless, Senator."

"It's atrocious, especially as the loss includes volunteer crews, spares, fuel, munitions and full backup facilities."

"It seems to be the day for losing things," said Sinter Pauls, consulting his notes. "No less than eight other Hub worlds have already anticipated similar losses. I make it a total of thirty four first-line fighting vessels plus support craft, all running apparently without registry or territorial insignia.'' He glanced at Liam slyly. ''Such a fleet would be a rare acquisition for any ugly and unscrupulous character who was planning on conducting his own war. Especially if he happened to be otherwise unemployed.''

''You are all mad, you understand?'' Liam was perilously near to tears as the magnitude of the plot unfolded in front of him. ''How long do you think Terra will be fooled by such a fiction?''

''Fiction? Surely these must be the insurgent forces Terra has been fighting for years?''

''Point taken!'' said Liam. ''But why do it this way?''

''Think about it. If the Hub worlds as a whole declared war on Terra only the destruction of the mother-planet could bring such a war to an end. But with an uncommitted strike force making the trouble-spots uncomfortable, Terra could well be forced to revise her policies at some point short of total war. In case you've missed the point, we're not being motivated by altruism.''

''I can see damn well what your motives are. If I start deploying a force like that against Terra, she won't need pick planetary quarrels to work off her surplus aggression. Liam's war will become a prime focus, right?''

''You're starting to get the idea,'' said Sinter Pauls slowly. ''Because you started with nothing, there is nothing you can ultimately lose. You can engage Terra in any way you choose, without being compromised by the necessity to have to defend a particular home-world. And should you win, you can withdraw without the necessity to raze the mother-planet.''

"You're crazy like a cockeyed fox, you understand? Thirty four extra ships against Terra's thousands isn't going to win anything. You're using me as a diversion and a cats-paw.''

"Read it any way you want. If you don't think you can handle it, say so. I'm sure we could find plenty of experienced commanders around the Hub who've a grudge against Terra. It just so happens you've already proven yourself to have the one advantage we can't better.''

"What's that?'' asked Liam Liam.

"You never bloody well admit you're beaten!'' said Sinter Pauls.

Outside the door Liam was met by Truman Wing Ai, who was handling technical liaison. Ai's face was grave.

"You've got troubles, Wing?''

"By the megabite. The lab's been working-over the apparatus on that ship you hijacked from Lightning. They've got the damn chamber working, but so far it's killed everything they've put into it.''

"Everything?''

"And everyone. That's a lethal instrument, Liam. After losing eight volunteers they had to desist for humanitarian reasons. Maybe the Terrans can make it work, but we don't appear to have captured any of the right technicians.''

"Damn! Their ghost warriors could be our Achilles heel. We *have* to crack that problem!''

"Well, the empirical approach isn't working. The labs want permission to dismantle the whole thing and re-work it from the basic theory up.''

"If we had a couple of years to spare, they'd be welcome. But how much leeway do you think Terra's going to allow us?"

"Months at most. Perhaps only weeks."

"Precisely, Wing! Dismantling's out of the question. I want that ghost-wagon checked out and readied for use. Ditto the mother ship used to transport it through tachyon space. You understand?"

"I understand the order, but not the reasoning behind it."

"It's simply this, Wing—if we don't have the time to learn to use it, we'll have to acquire somebody who already knows the answers. In the meantime, an issue of prayer-mats and heavy-duty worry beads would seem to be the best alternative."

CHAPTER XVI

Although his initial introduction to para-ion technique had been through Abel, the man's presence had not been very obvious throughout most of the training period. As Director, he occupied some high administrative position which did not bring him into direct contact with the trainees. Whilst there were other instructors also engaged in para-ion training, Dam's contact had been almost exclusively with Absolute; and Abel's authority only returned to the fore when Absolute declared her intention of putting Dam on experimental work.

The truth of the argument was never revealed, but for three days Dam did nothing at all, and the few glimpses he had of Absolute showed her to be in a mood of extreme and continuing anger. Rumour had it that Abel had wanted Dam transferred direct to combat duty, whilst Absolute was determined to use him for an experimental program. There was a long hiatus before Absolute got her way, although nobody doubted that she must finally win, because it was inconceivable that anybody could successfully oppose her regardless of their position in the organization. Nevertheless it was four days before Absolute came to collect Dam for further work.

"Get On your feet, Lover! You've caused me problems enough. Now you've to justify yourself, else you'll be in the front line of the fighting as fast as a translight ship can get you there."

"Do I detect opposition?" asked Dam guardedly.

She shrugged casually, but there was anger in the movement of her shoulders. "You were lucky. Something happened to a combat team which has thrown the emphasis right back on this type of development. Let's get started!"

Absolute led Dam to the huge furnace training environment in which he had had his first experience of the para-ion state. Although she was fully armed it was noticeable that no guards were called to accompany them. She made little noises of impatience as Dam struggled into his metal-mesh suit, then she set the pack on his back and adjusted the time delay.

"Ten minutes, Lover—and not a second more."

She hastened him to the paraformer and set it in operation with a haste which suggested that she herself had other things to do. Lacking any further instructions, Dam waited until the ion transition was complete, then made his way up the red-hot ramp into the white heat of the furnace chamber. This time the chamber was bare, all the clutter of the walls of the maze having been removed. However, the sheer brilliance and uniformity of the illumination and the lack of positive reference points to aid perspective, destroyed his orientation momentarily. Then as he sharpened his perception he stopped with a kind of shock: Absolute was there, also in para-ion state, but as a naked wraith, barely visible against the uniform incandescence of the furnace wall.

"Absolute?" Dam's initial reaction was that he was seeing some kind of trick projection. Firstly she had not had time to go through the paraformer and enter the chamber ahead of him. Secondly, she quite manifestly had neither mesh-suit nor information modulator pack on her completely unclothed form.

"What's the matter, Lover? Don't you believe what you see?"

Dam moved towards her, the better to see how her apparent situation was achieved; but the spectre which was Absolute slipped nimbly away from him, and, encumbered by his own suit and the pack, there was no way he could match her speed.

"If you're real, you're not conforming to what you've taught me about the principles of the para-ion state."

"I'm real enough, Lover—as real as anything can be in para-ion."

To emphasise her point she moved suddenly across and struck him a blow to the face with her hand. Although they were both para-ion analogues, the blow caught Dam hard, and he staggered and fell against the furnace wall.

"Satisfied?" she asked critically.

"I believe you," he said, regaining his feet. "Satisfaction would be something different again. I still don't see how you survive ion-state without a suit."

"You'll understand—later." There was an undercurrent of bitterness in her voice which the situation did nothing to explain. "But let's explore the advantages, Lover. Your records credit you with an expertise in unarmed combat which, given your size, I normally couldn't hope to match. But the advantage of the mobility given by the new process I am using should swing the advantage decidedly in my favour. We're here to put that proposition to the test.''

"You mean you want me to fight with you?''

"I'm not giving you the option. You're *going* to fight with me. As things are developing, we'll one day likely meet enemies with para-ion capability, in which case weaponry will be useless. It'll be hand against hand, man against man, with our new technique to give us the crucial advantage. You've eight minutes to reach the farther paraformer before your pack turns off.''

"So?''

"I intend to stop you reaching it, Lover. Which means you're fighting for your life. That's my assurance that you'll really try.''

She positioned herself between him and the exit, a nymph-like wraith, apparently as fragile as she was translucent; quite a different character from the dominant Absolute but not one bit the less dangerous. Her face was occupied by the same inexplicable passion which Dam had found there on other occasions when she was about to submit him to a grueling ordeal. With sharp memories of the past, Dam was under no illusions about the realities of his present predicament. To underestimate Absolute could easily be fatal.

He therefore took the initiative and began to move against her with an earnestness and intensity which was backed by the full weight of his former training in unarmed combat. However, the advantage was Absolute's right from the start. The restriction of the mesh suit and the modulator pack on his back told against him, whereas her easy mobility, enhanced by the para-ion state, made it virtually impossible for him to land a telling blow. Her retaliation, however, was cruel, and after a while her close approaches brought him such punishment that he was forced to retreat before her. Even more maddening was her look of vicious triumph as she expertly explored her advantage.

The only factor which turned the battle in his favour was his own growing sense of desperation as the seconds passed and the necessity for him to gain the paraformer became paramount. The knowledge of what was at stake turned him from a practised fighter into a dedicated killer, ignoring all pain and adversity in the single-minded intention of achieving his goal. The growing understanding that Absolute intended to keep him in the furnace chamber until his programed time had expired lent genius to his movements and brought unknown resources to power his muscles. Even so, it was only a mistake on the part of his adversary which permitted him to land the one blow which dropped her like a stone to the floor. He scooped her out of his way and literally hurled her prostrate body to one end of the chamber before leaping down the far ramp and reaching the paraformer with only seconds to spare.

Even here, Absolute had anticipated him. The transparent walls of the paraformer enclosure were already lowered, and nothing he could find to do would cause them to open and admit him. He watched the chronometer run to zero, and braced himself for violent dissolution as the pack switched off. When nothing happened, he retraced his way back to the furnace chamber, knowing that even his supposed deadline was one of Absolute's tricks. She was still on the floor, stirring feebly when he reached her, and he scooped her up and carried her down the slope by which he had entered the training environment, and laid her outside the paraformer whilst he made his painful transition back to the normal molecular state.

Absolute had made her own transition, and was waiting for him by the time that he emerged. The fact that she had been able to achieve reversion to molecular state without the need to use a paraformer was something which raised a line of speculation on Dam's brow. He conquered a desire to seize and hold her naked form, reading in the clinical intensity of her expression no sign that such a move would bring him anything but rebuff and punishment. Her uniform was nearby, and she began to dress slowly, but not before he had noticed that her body was completely unbruised despite the blows he had landed.

"Did you gain what you wanted?" he asked.

"For this part of the exercise, yes. If I can stop somebody with your fighting proficiency reaching a paraformer with a closing deadline, then I can stop virtually anything. So the technique's viable on two counts: greatly increased combat efficiency, and a freedom from dependence on a paraformer. We have the edge we need."

"Is it likely that anbody else has even started to develop the para-ion technique?"

"It's a certainty they will develop it. On Lightning the insurgents destroyed one paraformer ship and cleverly hijacked the reserve. With that plus their recent intelligence effort, it's only a matter of time before we meet them in the field.''

''What happened to the para-ion team on Lightning?''

''We lost every one of them. That's why Abel wanted you for immediate combat duty on a new team.''

''And you stopped him?''

''It was the Lightning incident which stopped him. To date we've lost three paraformer ships. It's the weak link in our operating system. This has put the emphasis back on the development of our new technique which doesn't require the use of a main paraformer at all. Apart from myself, you're to be the first to be equipped for it. Come, I want to show you something.''

Wonderingly, he followed her towards one of the laboratory blocks, overwhelmingly conscious of her femininity, yet still not daring to consider her objectively as a woman. He regarded her as a tormentress, yet his emotional involvement was secured by an overpowering fascination for this enigmatic and supremely capable female who so dominated his life.

In one of the laboratories she stopped before a round glass case of surgical cleanliness in which hung a suit of metal mesh. This was woven of filaments so fine that its texture was scarcely visible, and the material was so thin that light from behind penetrated it as easily as if it were no more than a shadow. For a few moments Dam stared at the ionsuit, wondering how and why it was different from the previous ones he had so reluctantly worn, and what was the purpose of this preview. He decided that the suit must be smaller and tighter—impossibly tight to judge from the finger diameter of the gloves and the detail of the body parts.

Absolute was watching his perlexity with critical amusement.

"That's your suit, Lover. Not only will it fit like a second skin—it is a second skin."

"I don't understand."

"You will! They're going to strip the skin off you surgically, dress you in the suit, then replace your natural skin. Once the nerve ends repair themselves through the mesh, you'll scarcely know its there—except that with the inclusion of an atom-powered paraformer implant you'll have inbuilt para-ion ability."

"Over my dead body!"

"Your dead body's no use to me, Lover. Your living body is. Don't think I'm giving you the option."

"There's no way I'm going to let you mutilate me by major surgery. You can kill me if you wish, but I'm not having that thing in my body. There's no point in continuing to live on those terms. Tell Abel I want to volunteer for active combat duty."

"I'll tell him you're a bloody coward."

"Cowardice doesn't figure. I'm bound to die anyway in para-ion service. But I'd sooner die as a natural man than live longer as a metal-skinned freak."

"Freak? God . . . I'll give you something to think about!"

She swiftly unbuttoned the blouse of her tunic again, shrugged the garment back, and thrust her bare torso close to him.

"Feel me! Come on—with your hands!"

Half afraid, he touched the soft, warm skin, then recoiled. Under the delicate, yielding flesh his sensitive fingers detected the deliberate weave of a metal mesh. His dismay brought a traumatic shock which numbed his arm.

"You . . .?" Too many conflicting things competed for the end of the sentence. "Why did you allow . . ."

"It's none of your bloody business. But if a woman can learn to live with it, so can you, Lover." She pulled her tunic blouse back abruptly. "I've laid the medics on for tomorrow."

"I'm serious, Absolute. Take what action you like against me, but in no way do I intend to become like you. Don't you realize it's warped your whole personality? I don't think it was only your skin they replaced with metal. I think they also stuffed your head full of barbed wire and rusty razor blades."

"You think so?" Although her face remained passive, there was a wealth of amused fury in her voice. "Don't get me started on what little boys are made of. You've not got the stomach to hear the answers. As it happens, Abel may still manage to steal you from me—but what *you* want has nothing to do with it. When you signed for para-ion service you transferred to us the power of life and death. But no mention was made of the quality of the life or the manner of death. So I'll promise you one thing, Lover—if I manage to keep you, what you've had to endure so far will be a mere nothing compared with what's to come."

It was the following morning before Dam gained any idea of what his fate was to be. He had slept badly and was still sadly tired when a guard awoke him and thrust a communicator set into his hand.

"Lover?" It was Absolute speaking on the radio link.

"Yes?"

"I've been discussing your case with Abel. I've been overruled, damn you. You're being transferred out for combat duty."

"That suits me fine! When do I go?"

"Immediately. There's a few formalities to be settled first, but after that you can go to hell by the shortest available route as far as I'm concerned. You'd better double over here and collect your training release right now, because I don't intend wasting any more time on you."

"I'm on my way."

Now that the chance for combat duty had become real, Dam was nowhere near as certain that he wanted it, but at least being outside the guarded walls of the training establishment would, he hoped, offered improved prospects for escape. Against this was the nagging suspicion that the self-contained para-ion ability offered by the suit beneath the skin formed the only possible escape route. Thinking about it carefully, it appeared to him that given what Absolute had demonstrated there was very little the guards could bring against him were he so equipped. Removing the need for the cumbersome machinery of the paraformer had removed the last obstacle to crashing the camp's defences while in the para-ion condition. Nothing in his psyche, however, could accept the prospect of living with the metal mesh beneath his skin.

The guard escorted him to the polished hall outside Absolute's office. Dam knocked mechanically.

"Come!" said Absolute's voice, and even the single word seemed to signal her frustration.

He entered, but even as he cleared the door he knew he had made a mistake. White-clad arms were waiting on either side to seize and carry him forward to where Absolute, with a face of malicious triumph, was waiting for him with an anaesthetic pad. Sudden panic drove Dam into a frenzy, but he was in the hands of experts, and though he summoned all the strength available to him, his face was thrust inexorably towards the fatal pad. His last impression was that of Absolute's golden nails thrusting an.ersatz moon towards his face, and the sickly scalding of the anesthetic in his lungs.

He woke later to find himself strapped on a hospital trolley. A burst of fear made him strain to break his bonds, but they were too secure. His movements brought Absolute over to look down on him, and once again Dam saw the inexplicable passion in her expression. She was both the goddess who mocked his agonies and the controller of his future; yet his hatred for her was infused with a large measure of desire, and his fear of her was similarly complicated by a near-masochistic fascination. Both psychologically and physically, Dam knew her influence on him would remain until the day of his death.

Someone came to wheel the trolley, and Absolute walked in front. He could not see her, but the sound of her steel-tipped heels on the floor seemed to speak the thought that was uppermost in his mind:

"*Bitch! Bitch! Bitch! Bitch! Bitch!* . . ." all the way down the echoing corridors to the operating theatre.

CHAPTER XVII

In many respects Lightning had been more fortunate than many of the other worlds Terra had chosen to attack. The defenders normal mode of living, massively insulated from the great storms which racked the planet's surface, had caused them to develop living conditions incidentally well suited to withstand all but the most dedicated space bombardment. Their extensive use of tunnels deep beneath the mountains rendered most of their installations proof against even nuclear attacks. Furthermore, the rising generations had grown to accept the violence of the planetary atmosphere as part of their natural environment; whereas units of the Terran occupation force had no such background, and viewed the dark and turbulent wastes of the surface as a region akin to Hell.

A further factor working in favour of the defenders of Lightning was the fact that, owing to her relative isolation even from the Hub communities, very little was known either about the size of her population or its distribution. Although a military government had been installed, the deposed planetary administration had so successfully sabotaged the record systems that whole townships, especially some of the submarine food-farm complexes and subterranean mining colonies, had remained effectively unknown to the new rulers. The smallness of the cities had led the Terrans into the error of believing the entire population was probably less than fifty million. A true count which would include the small enclaves scattered around the black and jagged coastlines would have returned a figure nearly four times as great. The magnitude of the error was due to the Terrans habitual assumption that most people live in cities: it needed long familiarity with the way of life on Lightning to appreciate that on the planet of storms the reverse was true.

The apparent pockets of resistance against which the Terrans had moved their lost ghost-squad had in fact been deliberately contrived by Garside Raad, and the main elements of the real resistance force had been persuaded to remain concealed against the time of Liam Liam's promised return to give them some coverage from space. Nobody, least of all the inhabitants of Lightning, held any illusions about the full weight of the holocaust which would arrive if the commander of the ships in orbit decided to seek the ultimate solution to the Lightning 'problem' and put a few planet-breaking hellburners down on the surface. Thus the Terrans were pacified by an uneasy simulation of conquest; while beneath, around and above them, shadowy forces were being carefully arranged.

Such was the subtlety of these forces that the action actually began not near to Lightning but halfway towards Terra, where the communications ship handling the FTL relay link between Terra and the Hub reported intruders in her sector of space, and appealed for assistance. Shortly a report was broadcast that the intruders had passed without incident, and that assistance was no longer required. Units of a Terran ship-chain which had started to her aid were recalled: had they continued, they would have found the original relay ship totally destroyed, and sitting in its place, expertly concerned with handling the traffic for the Terran FTL relay, was a new ship without any territorial insignia. So efficiently had this substitution been arranged that nobody but those concerned with its planning and execution knew that it had taken place.

Having lost his superior in Liam Liam's earlier attack, the Terran reserve commander, Ernst Rimini, was unsurprised to receive notification of the pending arrival of a new sector commander. Painfully aware of the shortcomings of his own performance—he had lost both paraformer ships and an entire para-ion squad—Rimini had already resigned himself to the prospect of demotion and posting to some more hazardous occupation. In this frame of mind he was not as diligent as he might have been in counter-checking the identity of the approaching vessel which bore his new superior. The personal credentials he did check via the communications relay data link were speedily confirmed by a message appearing to originate from Terra; and thus he greeted Sector Commander Mail without once wondering why the Terran insignia of his stateship stood on a vessel of obvious Hub design.

Sector Commander Mail was an unusual man, with a slight outworld accent which might have been more consciously called to attention had he not been so engagingly ugly and had such a deep and penetrating mind that the luckless Rimini was immediately forced to defend every single action he had taken. The interview lasted six hours, after which Rimini, believing himself to be in complete disgrace, was ordered to begin his immediate return to Terra for re-assignment. With the bitter heart of a man who knows he has wasted a life's career, the reserve commander transferred to a fast cruiser, and ordered it back towards Terra and the Rim.

Breaking with tradition, Sector Commander Mail did not immediately call a shipboard conference of fleet captains, but instead required executive officers to locate any survivors or technicians from the former para-ion project. Such was the apparent logic behind the move that protocol was forgotten, and the sole remnants of the ill-fated 'ghost' team—seven members of the technical crew who had been visiting supply ships during the hijack episode—were swiftly located and transferred to the sector commander's stateship.

It was only at this point that Mail set up a full shipboard conference on the acting flagship, to which he required attendance not only by the fleet captains and their seconds, but also the senior officers commanding the ground forces. Such a demand was unprecedented, but held promise of mammoth policy changes in the conduct of the Lightning campaign, and was therefore doubly welcome. There was scarcely an absentee when the assembly gathered on the flagship and settled to greet their new sector commander. Their anticipation was short-lived, however, because an unaccountable explosion entirely destroyed the ship and all who were within her.

Stunned and virtually leaderless, the remainder of the orbiting warforce hastily regrouped, and sent a message via the FTL link to report their plight to Terra and seek instructions. Within an hour the reply came: 'Suspend all operations against Lightning. Await reinforcements.' Needless to say, the answer did not originate from Terra, but from an unidentified ship in the relay chain; nor did Terra herself receive any information which might lead her to doubt in the satisfactory progress of the Lightning campaign. The orbiting warforce sat back to await reinforcements, having no idea how long these might take to come.

Meanwhile, the stateship which had brought the fatal sector commander to the scene had slipped almost casually out of orbit and made planetfall in a sheltered bowl in a broken range above Bama. Under the lashing ferocity of the storm, the Terran insignia began to wash away to reveal faintly beneath the overlay its original name of *Starbucket*. Through the pitiless punishment of the elements ran Liam Liam, who bore more than a passing resemblance to the former sector commander who was presumed to have been killed when the flagship exploded. The similarity was completed by the fact that the former agent was covering his head with a uniform jacket which bore the crests, stars and medals with which normally only Terran sector commanders were adorned.

Under an overhang which concealed the entrance to a fortified tunnel, Garside Raad, apparently much aged by his experiences with the Terran occupation force, was only too glad to see Liam, but there was a question hanging over his brow.

"Well met, Liam! How're things upstairs?"

"In orbit? The nearest approach to chaos which can be devised. We eliminated most of the local top brass in that last space-blast, and we're intercepting all of their signalling with Terra and modifying some of their instructions to suit ourselves."

"That's even better than I'd hoped. So what brings you back here?"

"To deliver a few words of wisdom. The situation in orbit can't last for long. Whatever Terrans may be, they aren't stupid. Soon they'll have a task force out here to investigate. When that force gets here, I think the retribution will be massive."

"But we've time to drive the occupying force off first?"

"Certainly, if that's the way you want to play it. But the more damage you do to them now, the worse they'll make it for you in the end, you understand? I can give you some coverage from space, but I can't fight a Terran armada."

"But what's the alternative?"

"Co-operate. Play helpful and subservient to your Terran masters currently in distress. Blame all their misfortunes on the Devil's disciple called Liam Liam, and hope like hell they fall for it."

"Are you serious?"

"I only tell you the truth, you understand? These are early days in the history of opposition to Terra. If you fight them now, they will crush you. Acquiesce, and many of you will live to see more equal battles."

"Liam, even if I wanted to, I couldn't hold our people now. It's fight first and pay the Devil later. You know that."

"That's what I figured you'd say. It's the real reason I held on. During my brief career as Terran sector commander I made it my business to establish what they had in the way of planetary hellburners up there in orbit. Well, they've seven, all in one hellship which they keep in far orbit for safety. That's enough to destroy all life on Lightning about twenty times over. If you carry the fight against the ground forces and look like winning, they're just nervous to put one or two of them down here."

"It's a prospect we've already faced. But we'll fight them nevertheless."

"The good patriot isn't the one who dies defending his territory, it's the one who makes the enemy die whilst attacking it, you understand?"

"Meaning what?"

"That I can't subscribe to heroics, however motivated. War's too deadly a game to be controlled by sentiment. If you want any further assistance from me, I'll need a solemn promise."

"Name it."

"As I attempt to make my exit through the ship chain, I shall try to take that hellship out of space. If I succeed, you'll be in no doubt of it, because the flash will be as brilliant as a thousand suns. But if I fail, those weapons will still be poised above you. In that case I want your solemn promise not to attack, but meekly to sit it out until we can meet Terra on more equal terms."

"That's a ferocious demand to make, Liam."

"It's all I have to offer, you understand?"

Garside Raad considered in silence for a moment.

"I can't promise more than the intent. I don't know if even I could hold the population of Lightning passive under the Terran heel."

"I'll settle for good intentions," said Liam Liam. "And may God have charge of all our futures!"

It was probable that the demoralization of the orbiting warforce added to the success of the mystery surrounding the return of the former sector commander's stateship from the planet's surface: whatever the reason, the little ship regained its place in orbit without once having to answer a challenge, although its mission had been the cause of much speculation. Even though the sector commander was himself presumed dead, the impression he had left on the few with whom he had actually spoken made it seem an impertinence even to question the captain of his vessel. It was rumoured that Mail had in fact been on a mission of galactic importance, and that his pose as sector commander had been an elaborate, and unsuccessful, attempt to divert the attention of interstellar espionage agents. Euken Tor, commanding the little ship, made only the formal, routine communications with the rest of the fleet, thereby neither confirming or denying these suspicions.

When the unexpected happened, none of those concerned with the maintenance of fleet security were prepared for it, or knew how to react when the details became apparent. The stateship had gradually drifted until it had assumed one of the outermost orbits of the fleet proper, a position it occupied for many hours in apparent quiescence. Then abruptly it began to transmit urgent distress signals, and at the same time its powerful motors broke into life and began to fling it tangentially away from the orbital ring.

Analysing some drastic powerplant runaway, or possibly even sabotage, the security ships watched in fascination as the small craft accelerated at a truly amazing rate and careered off wildly towards the deeps of space, all the time appealing frenziedly for an assistance which none of the parked vessels were able to supply. The main drama came with the horrified realization that if the little ship continued its present trajectory, its path would bring it remarkably close to the hellship, way out in its safety orbit.

At this point it was seriously questioned whether the stateship shoud be taken out of space by weaponry before the hellship was endangered. By the time a decision had been made, it was already too late to attempt to destroy the fleeting craft. The dilemma was resolved by the little ship itself: as it passed the diabolical carrier it revealed some very superior weaponry and the subsequent radiation flare blacked-out even the most discriminating scanners and instruments in the warfleet, causing temporary and permanent blindness to many human observers. In the circumstances, the exact course of events could never be determined, but it was certain that after the plasma cloud had cooled sufficiently to permit an examination of the scene, both the hellship and the stateship were no longer to be seen. In any case, the point became academic, because the ground forces on Lightning were already reporting massive attacks by insurgents who were beginning to overwhelm their defences.

CHAPTER XVIII

When Dam awoke he experienced an almost total lack of sensation from his epidermis. He was not bandaged, but laying inside a sterile plastic tent on a kind of water bed, with his whole body being periodically bathed with a heavy fog from diffusers above and around him. He needed only to lift one arm and view its sickly whiteness and the lacework of a hundred cuts to know that the operation had been performed as promised.

The knowledge raised in him a feeling of nausea and sick resignation, that should have been countered by a tide of anger—but surgical shock, probably compounded by the judicious use of drugs, had robbed him of the will to fight; he relaxed back onto the trembling water bed and consciously willed himself to sleep, hoping never again to wake.

Yet wake he did, with no knowledge of how many hours or days had passed. The aseptic fog had ceased, and with the gradual drying of the skin a semblance of his normal flesh tone was returning. The multiple incisions were now reduced to the faintest white tracery which promised soon to disappear, so fine and skillful had been the surgery. There was no outward sign that the suit now lay beneath his skin, but his imagination broadly—and wrongly— suggested the outlines of the mesh which his eyes could not discern.

Experimentally he moved one hand to touch the other, then immediately wished he had not done so, for where flesh touched flesh there arose a sensation of a painful, crawling fire where severed nerve ends were regaining their old function with considerable protest at the dislocation. Thereafter he lay very still, attempting not to spread the excruciating sensation to other parts of his body. He was not successful. The flame spread slowly up his arms and began to tear at his chest. A medic looked in and started the fog again, which gave Dam some relief; then came Absolute, who had the fog turned off, and who returned periodically to watch him inscrutably through the fabric of the tent.

During one of her periods of absence, the tent was removed, and Dam was given an injection of something which muted the pain while leaving him drowsily conscious. When Absolute returned there was a furious argument, and finally she came over and sat on the edge of the bed.

"It's unfair, Lover, that they should make it so easy for you!"

"Easy!" Even under the drugs Dam reacted.

"When it was done to me, no drugs were allowed. It was experimental, you see. They were doubtful if all the nerve ends would repair, and wished to monitor the progress of the pain to see if it was containable. It wasn't—but that didn't stop them.

When the agony drove me berserk, they simply tied me down and let it continue.''

"Is that why you don't feel pain now?" Dam asked.

"Of course I feel it, Lover—probably more acutely than you. But when it continues at such levels, you either have to learn to contain it or go mad. You're going to have the opportunity to learn to handle it, as I did. It does marvelous things for the character."

"I don't think 'marvelous' is quite the word, Absolute. They've twisted you inside."

"You're wrong, Lover. One day you'll understand. To aid that understanding, I've forbidden them to give you any more pain killers. I want you to go through the same barrier I did."

Dam's torment lasted about a week, during which time, had they allowed it, he would have torn off his own skin in maddened attempts to relieve the intolerable fire which consumed him. Then gradually the burning faded to an itch, and the itch gave way to a tactile sensitivity which was somehow heightened by the newness of the re-connections the nerves had made through the flesh. With this sensitivity came also an acceptance of the subcutaneous suit and a loss of the sense of loathing and self-disgust which the presence of the artifact had originally induced. At last he was able to deny that he was any less of a man because of the suit's inclusion. He adopted the feeling that he had become a man *plus* something; the full potential of which had to be explored.

In the soft flesh of his waist, between the hip and the rib cage, his fingers could detect that small packages had been implanted on both sides. Each sat deeply, causing him no discomfort. He suspected that one of them was the nuclear-electric capsule that powered the paraforming process and the other was the micro-miniature modulator pack responsible for maintaining his identity while in the para-ion state.

When Absolute came to observe his final check-out by the medics, she adopted an extremely professional and impersonal approach. For the first time Dam saw the dichotomy between her astuteness as a para-ion technician and the complexities of character which motivated her. He thought he could detect no less than three different aspects of Absolute: the clinically cool technologist; the quick, critical, and occasionally sadistic mentor of para-ion techniques; and beneath all this a feminine base-character almost frighteningly powerful in the strength of its emotions. He did not know whether or not these divisions were figments of his imagination, but one thing was certain: he no longer felt resentment at the way she had left him to suffer, because out of that overwhelming agony he had begun to understand the real lesson she was trying to teach him—how to acquire that hideous inner strength that no ordinary circumstance could conquer.

Later they went to the heated-hydrogen furnace, by-passed the paraformer, and went as close as they dared to the foot of the red-hot entry ramp. Here Absolute showed Dam the radio-pulse apparatus, little larger than a small book, with which the paraformer package in his body could be activated. The actual transition was no less agonizing for being self-contained, but now Dam found he could lean towards the sensation and accept the pain with an almost savage joy, as a swimmer can enjoy a plunge into icy water and rejoice in its tonic embrace, while lesser spirits are shattered by the numbing cold.

In para-ion state, he ran ahead of her into the furnace chamber, his body adopting the para-hydrogen identity of the environment, which left his as a shadowy wraith in the tide of red-hot gas. Absolute had a new trick to demonstrate. By using the enclosure chamber and gas supply of the paraformer, but not its coils, she managed to achieve a transition into para-sodium. When she reached the heated chamber, the ionised sodium lit radiantly with a brilliant yellow flare; like an immortal, naked sure goddess, she went to torment her shadowy acolyte in the bright-red regions of an artificial Hell.

Absolute flicked the paper across the desk. Dam read it curiously but without gleaning much information from its coded jargon. The order was signed by Abel himself.

"What does it mean?" he asked.

"It means, Lover, that the honeymoon is over. Abel finally got his own way, and a new para-ion team is to be formed from the advanced trainees here. You and I are both included, because we need to study the subcutaneous-suit technique in the field."

"Which field?"

"A minor Hub world called Syman. Do you know it?"

"I know of it. But most of your para-ion team is comprised of former Hub men. What makes you think you can make us fight our own kind?"

"It's simple, really! You're all dedicated survivors, else you'd not have survived the training this far. When you go out on a mission you're put into some particularly nasty para-ion identity such as phosphorus. Either you fight as directed, or we don't admit you back through the paraformer. With men like yourselves, with such a well-developed sense of self-preservation, we seldom have trouble. Potential rebels are self-eliminating. Rather neat, don't you think?''

"It's the diabolical product of a set of sick minds," said Dam sourly.

"Come, Lover! You're a soldier. Do you need me to teach you about the ethics of war and conquest? The prize goes always to those best fitted to seize and hold it; the weaklings go to the wall. That's a fundamental fact of life.''

"Fighting for survival is one thing," said Dam. "But fighting without necessity, to ensure others may not survive, is an insane perversion. In no way do the Hub worlds threaten Terra's existence. Only her craving for dominance is at stake. So we're talking about the maintenance of power mania, not the ethics of war.''

"I said you'd a lot to understand, Lover. Some of us need to fight just to stay alive, else we atrophy and die. And this happens with societies no less than with people. That's the principle behind all human history; conquer or you will fall, either from external enemies or from creeping paralysis within.''

Two hovertrucks came for them that same evening. Twelve men, Dam and Fiendish among them, were herded into one truck, while Absolute and a party of officers rode in the other. They were taken to a military spaceport, where the pads were dominated

154

by an armed spacecruiser, one of the most wicked-looking war machines Dam had ever seen. It was not to this vessel, though, that the party was directed. Behind the cruiser, a craft-carrier stood nearly as high as the warcraft but fat with its cargo, which Dam guessed to be two paraformer ships.

The carrier and the cruiser made a simultaneous blast-off from the pads, and it was obvious that the function of the warcraft was to act as a diligent escort to the carrier mother-ship so pregnant with her spiteful spawn. Such an over-protective arrangement made Dam raise his eyebrows. It hinted that the para-ion team and its associated operating vessels was a facility worth guarding even at such an extreme cost as that involved in dedicating a major warcraft to the task. It further suggested that the Terrans were at last encountering serious opposition from the Hub. Of all the things that had happened to him since he had left Castalia, this latter notion was the only one that gave Dam any hope.

CHAPTER XIX

"And I tell you that Terra's attack on Syman isn't quite the idiocy it appears," said Euken Tor.

"I never said otherwise, you understand? But I'd be interested to hear your reasoning. Don't underestimate the fact that strategically, Syman is the source of most of the nickel-iron used for shipbuilding around that sector of the Hub."

"That's the point I don't buy, Liam. Do you know how they distribute that stuff? They mine it in hundred tonne slabs which are then hauled into planetary orbit by slow tugs. From there the slingships net the slabs and accelerate them up to a tenth of the speed of light before casting loose. The slingships return for the next load, while the slabs make their own way a full two light years distance to be picked up by the catch-ships feeding the foundries on Toroliver."

"Interesting, but I fail to see the relevance, you understand?"

"Then you've not considered its implications. At any moment there's around a twenty year supply of nickel-iron slabs already in transit through space. If

Syman ceased production tomorrow, the foundaries on Toroliver would still have about two decades in which to look for an alternative supply; the strategic value of Syman is largely an illusion.''

"You could equally say that neither Rigon nor Lightning were of direct strategic importance to the Hub. They came under Terra's guns for reasons of prestige and colonial blackmail.''

"True, but each had relatively large populations, and therefore greater propaganda value. That isn't true for Syman, which has only a mining community of about ten thousand. There are perhaps another thousand in the sling-ships and space ancillaries, but in galactic terms, who would even miss them?''

"I would, you understand? But I think you were about to make your point.''

"Syman is nothing but a ball of nickel-iron. It has no external atmosphere, and no surface installations. Aside from the space ancillaries, the entire population lives deep-sealed in the internal cavities left by the mining work. In short, it's a place suited *par excellance* for resisting damage by space bombardment. In theory, it's about the most difficult proposition Terra could have chosen. About the only way Syman could be taken is by a Terran para-ion squad.''

"That agrees with my own analysis.''

"Then it raises an interesting question. Knowing how precious their ion-warriors are to them, why are they deploying them against so worthless a target? I suggest they are hoping to gain the head of their favourite enemy. To me, Syman smells like a Liam-trap.''

"Ah!'' Liam Liam leaned back in his chair, "A

good point, Euken. You've filled in a piece of the puzzle which was missing. I'd been so busy considering what were the advantages we could gain from Syman, that I'd not stopped to consider the converse.''

''What are the possible advantages of Syman to us?''

''When we removed our relay ship from the Terran communications chain, the truth about Lightning managed to reach Terra. They've since had time to digest what occurred, and to complete their plans to stop it happening again. Intelligence reports suggest there's a new paraformer mother-ship already out from Terra bound for Syman. If they have developed an answer to our tactics, that ship contains it. It's vital we know what they've got aboard her.''

''So we can't afford to opt out of the Syman operation even if we do suspect a trap?''

''Not if we're to stay in the race, you understand? I think now that that ship may even be both bait and jaws for the trap. Any word from Truman Wing Ai?''

''A message just came in. With the information gained from the Terrans you captured in the second Lightning episode, the labs have managed to crack the paraformer problem, although the treatment's decidedly rough. Wing reckons that if pushed, he could get a dozen volunteers into para-ion state, but he's not too confident he could get them all out again. He's pleading for more time to experiment.''

''The Terran mother-ship's already on her way. That defines the time we have available. Tell Wing I want our own para-ion squad, and I want them yesterday. If the Terrans are planning to surprise us, it's only fair we prepare a few surprises of our own.''

For reasons known only to themselves, the Terrans carefully maintained their fictional charge of insurrection against the mining planet of Syman. Even though a fearsome warforce was placed in a close and threatening orbit around the metal world, they did not immediately interrupt trade, but insisted on a series of meetings with the planetary council in which their threats and charges and demands became more outrageous and more ominous. Meanwhile the great elevators continued to rise to the surface bearing the gigantic slabs of nickel-iron which were expertly grappled by the slow tugs and hauled into low orbit for pickup by the sling-ships.

There was also a lesser volume of trade in the reverse direction. While sufficient oxygen could be won from the oxide traces in the mined metal to secure the life-maintaining element in the recycled internal atmosphere, no source of nitrogen was available as a dilutent. The nitrogen came from two light years distance in huge shuttle containers which, once having been accelerated by the Toroliver sling-ships, made their own way to the vicinity of Syman, there to be caught by the two catch-ships maintained for the purpose. Base nutrients for the hydroponic gardens, planned with a twenty year delivery delay in mind, also travelled the same route, leaving to the occasional FTL starships the carriage only of people and the more urgent, intricate and exotic goods for the metal world.

There was no way by which it could have been

externally distinguished, but one of the shuttles which the Syman catch-ships netted from a grazing approach and shepherded through the ship-chain to the elevator platforms on the surface was completely untypical of a normal incoming catch load. Although it had come in close to one of the usual freight trajectories, the shuttle had been in flight not for twenty years, but for only a few days, and from a distance only just beyond the scanner range of the Terran warfleet. Its second peculiarity was that the shuttle cylinder contained not liquid nitrogen, as its manifest declared, but the small paraforming ship that had been hijacked from Lightning. Smuggled swiftly away from the elevator shaft and skilfully concealed in a specially prepared mine gallery, there could have been no reason for the Terrans to even suspect that such a vessel had been concealed deep in the planet's guts.

With the ship had come a mass of communications equipment and twenty men, eight of them technicians from Wing Ai's laboratories, eleven hand-picked Hub commandos, and Liam Liam. Most of the men were slightly grim-faced, with a full understanding of the difficulties and dangers with which the venture was fraught. Only Liam Liam rode the tensions and pressures with equanimity, and this was said to be because, with him, living at an extreme pitch of danger was a normal mode of life.

For those who had never before visited Syman, the metal world was an unexpected and fascinating place. Stripped by some cosmic holocaust of its former mantle, Syman was the solid metal core of some far greater planet. Now it was nothing more than a gigantic ball of metal into which, like sophisticated space-maggots, the miners had driven their shafts and galleries.

The fascination arose from the fact that their towns, their apartments, their furniture, and virtually everything they used or possessed were all constructed from nickel-iron. Faced with the challenge of extreme monotony, their craft workshops had been diligent in exploring design and finishes, and their engineers and architects had achieved levels of sheer genius in cutting cavities of marvellous complexity and intriguing design, so that the turning of every corner revealed a new vista of marvels wrought in polished metal, and even the most mundane of rooms held artifacts of great artistry and beauty of design. Imported coloured materials were always circumspectly used to enhance the native forms, and although the business of Syman was gross metal mining, the effect was of this being performed in a palace of silvery, oriental splendour.

Liam Liam was less concerned with the marvels of the place than he was with communication and aspects of defence. The great elevator shafts which provided the only access to the surface, had multiple airlock systems to prevent the escape of even minute amounts of the precious recycled atmosphere; and in order to avoid the zone of temperature variation as Syman spun between its sun and the coldness of space, there were no horizontal galleries less than two kilometres deep in the solid metal. In company with Syman's Security Councillor, he completed his inspection with the conviction that no weapon-violence short of a hellburner could destroy the installation. The elevator platforms themselves were the weakest points, but constructed as they were to handle hundred tonne slabs of metal for despatch, and even whole sling-ships for transit to the repair bays, these were super-massive pieces of engineering by any standards.

Communications were more difficult. Because of the shielding effect of the great metal mass of the planet, transmission of space signals from inside Syman was impossible. For regular commercial communications, the planetary ball itself was used both as receiving and transmitting antenna, a purpose for which it functioned admirably. However, there was no method by which the transmissions could be reduced to the tight beam that Liam would have preferred to give his transmissions the requisite security. There was no answer to this problem short of drilling a new shaft through two kilometres of nickel-iron to the surface. Liam had finally to arrange his transmitters in the knowledge that everything he sent to the *Starbucket* far out in space could be easily jammed or monitored by the Warforce above. It was a grave deficiency, and one that could easily prove fatal if the Terrans realized the nature of the coded data, and applied it to their own battle intelligence.

Soon Liam's scoutships were reporting the paraformer mother-ship and her formidable escort nearing the space approaches to Syman. The importance of their arrival to the Terrans could be deduced by their placing their whole fleet on standby alert, and by the immediate prohibition placed on the movement of the sling-ships which had previously been free to move their gross cargoes through the Terran orbital ring. The sling-ships were allowed to remain in an outer orbit, however, presumably because, being unarmed and unshielded, they could be shot out of space at any time their presence became inconvenient. In point of fact, having gained high orbit, most of them chose to wander off into space. The Terran invaders missed the fact that the several sling-ships who remained had been equipped with Liam's cameras and scanners, and that interwoven with the commercial and technical chatter of the communications with the planetary base was a multiplexed information channel which was feeding Liam with a bird's-eye view of the ship chain in orbit far above his head.

As Liam had predicted, the Terrans lost no time in releasing a paraforming ship from the carrier once parking orbit had been achieved; and the deployment of the remaining fighting vessels made it a certainty that the trick of harassment by jumping out of tachyon space for a sneak attack, which Liam's little force had previously employed, would have been disasterous had it been attempted near Syman. The Terrans were learning fast, and their tactical judgment was sound. So effectively had they covered all the angles that Liam began to have just a hint of doubt about whether they could also have anticipated the presence of a second para-ion squad dedicated to fighting Liam's war. As the Terran paraformer ship plunged towards the surface he became even more convinced that Euken's notion of a Liam trap stood a good chance of becoming a reality.

CHAPTER XX

From Terra to Syman's orbit via tachyon-space jumps was a thirty-day journey. Absolute and the other officers had transferred by pinnace to the accompanying cruiser early in the flight, leaving only a guard detail to maintain order. The crew of the craft-carrier seemed unaware of the aspects of enforcement surrounding the presence of the para-ion crew; and Dam, having no flight duties to perform, found his movements around the carrier were unrestricted. In company with the wild-eyed Fiendish, he took the opportunity to examine the carrier and the two paraformer craft contained in the craft-lock. Such an interest appeared to arouse no comment either with the crew or the guards, and was presumably thought to be dutiful familiarization with the equipment in preparation for the coming encounter.

A knowledge of the equipment at the training base made it evident to the two explorers that the paraformer ships were aptly named, being little more than paraforming units plus ancillary services built into small spacecraft not much larger than the little

pinnaces themselves. Such was the weight and size
of the installation that the compact design had only
been achieved by omitting the conventional
tachyon-space capability from the little ships. This
explained the use of the craft-carrier to transport
them over interstellar distances.

Fiendish was analyzing the situation with an eye
to the possibility of escape. Dam, who as a space-
army officer already knew something of the nature of
Syman from the navigational hazards created by the
Syman-Toroliver sling shuttle, was less hopeful. An
escape to Syman, he suggested, was only the exchange of one dungeon for another if the Terrans
were contemplating occupation of the metal world.
For himself he was content to explore and to attempt
to understand all of the equipment he countered,
knowing that such background information might
prove invaluable when he judged the time right to
make his own move.

Unable to persuade Dam to join him, Fiendish left
him and went to try to enlist support amongst other
members of the para-ion squad. Dam continued his
detailed examination of one of the paraforming ships
and its contents. Ultimately he made a discovery
which was both logical and at the same time unexpected: in a locked cupboard he found not one but
several of the little radio-pulse units with which
Absolute had activated both his and her own inbuilt
para-ion capabilities. Not daring to believe his luck,
he inspected both instruments closely. They appeared to belong to two groups, and were probably
sets of individually tunes radio-activators, each set
matched to a particular individual. Since, on the

information Absolute had given to him, only she and himself were yet so equipped, it seemed logical to assume that they had one set each. But which was his?

He took the radio units out carefully and laid them on a table, trying to find any marks or figures which might give him a clue to the identity of the person who would be affected by the actuation. He was uncomfortably aware that without a knowledge of the range of the transmissions if he mistakenly operated the unit attuned to Absolute he could well trigger her prematurely into a para-ion state even if she was in the accompanying cruiser. This would both betray his interest and no doubt raise a considerable degree of anger against him.

He could decide nothing from the coding pattern on the boxes, but one of them had a surface shine slightly dulled, as if by repeated handling; that one, he decided, must belong to Absolute. He therefore selected an activator from the other group, arranged the rest back in the cupboard, and, holding his breath, he pressed the operating button.

It was a painful transition, but beautifully swift. Since no other forming material had been supplied, he had automatically adopted the identity of the air around him; in the para-ion form of a dull lilac ghost he prowled the interior of the little ship, trying to come to terms with the potential involved in having complete access to the para-ion state. He had found how the timing mechanism worked, and allowed himself ample time in which to experiment. On hearing close footsteps approaching, however, he hastily thrust the timer back to zero, and hoped fervently that he had understood the principles of its operation sufficiently to ensure a swift and safe return to his normal molecular identity.

He was still reeling from the reorientation shock when Absolute came through the door. So closely timed was her entry that Dam felt she must have seen the para-ion glow as she came in from the docking ramp, but she showed neither curiosity nor surprise at finding him in the little ship, and if she noticed anything unusual, she gave no sign of it.

"Well met, Lover! We make orbit around Syman in about eight hours. I wanted to discuss our part in this."

"I'd just as soon sit this one out, if it's all the same to you."

She shot him a quick look of mock disapproval.

"It's not all the same to me, Lover! We've just completed details of the para-ion campaign against Syman. Eleven men plus one officer trained in the old technique will make a normal para-ion approach, descending in a paraformer ship. Shortly behind them, and with maximum fleet coverage, we two will make planetfall in a pinnace ostensibly as part of a non para-ion commando follow-up. The para-ion squad will make the initial breach for us. We will stay in normal molecular identity until we're actually inside the installation."

"Wouldn't it be safer if we went straight down in para-ion state with the others?"

"Not necessarily. The fact is that we're expecting them to meet some fairly sophisticated opposition, though we don't yet know what form it might take. So we two are an unsuspected para-ion reserve, with capabilities the opposition hasn't yet encountered. Our intervention could well be crucial to the whole encounter.''

"Sophisticated opposition on Syman? Don't you know what Syman is?''

"I know exactly what Syman is. But it's not just Syman we're up against. There's a Hub guerrilla group with a special line of dirty tricks.''

"Guerilla's don't have para-ion capability.''

"These may have. To date they've destroyed two para-former ships and hijacked a third. They betrayed their special interest when they returned and kidnapped seven para-ion technicians from the fleet around Lightning.''

"And you think they'll field their own para-ion troops on Syman?''

"We don't know what they'll do, but Syman was selected as being the ideal scene for such a confrontation, because under no circumstances can they win. If they think they can master the para-ion technique, Lover, they're about to learn reality the hard way. And don't run away with any crazy ideas about trying to join the opposition. Your para-ion identity will be entirely under my control. You will react and fight exactly as directed, otherwise it will take no more than my finger on a button to eliminate you painfully and finally. You know me well enough to know I wouldn't hesitate.''

"I love you too!'' said Dam sourly, rising to his feet because the interview appeared to be at an end.

Absolute had turned away from him and was attending to the contents of the cupboard from which he had taken the radio pulse unit. The missing unit now rested seemingly large and heavy in his pocket, and he judged it to be only a matter of seconds before she realized that one was missing, and was drawn to the obvious conclusion. Nevertheless he forced himself to walk away with studied nonchalance, and the vicious shout which should have accompanied the discovery did not come.

The pinnace containing Absolute, Dam and a commando group dropped out of orbit fourteen minutes after the departure of the paraformer ship. Most of the intervening time had been taken up by the descent of the para-ion squad to the surface, and at the time of the pinnace's departure very little resistance had been reported. For the duration of their own descent they closely monitored the reports of the para-ion men and followed their progress in taking over the elevator control system. Then at a certain point, all transmissions on the para-ion squad's radio channel stopped.

The radio blackout was not unexpected. As the attackers had penetrated deeper into the metal ball, so their own transmissions would have been increasingly intercepted and absorbed by the bulk of the metal world. It was not anticipated that further word would be obtained until the para-ion men had gained control of one of the main transmitters which used the planetary ball itself as a transmitting aerial. Even so it was highly disconcerting for those in the second ship to be unable to ascertain the fate of those who had gone before.

Space-suited, the occupants of the pinnace leaped out onto Syman's surface near one of the great elevator platforms, and ran towards the elevator-control dome, which had been captured by the first para-ion team. A para-ion man had been assigned to operate the platform that had taken his comrades below. He had been quick to tell the newcomers how, once having descended with the para-ion squad, the platform had returned to the surface and thereafter refused to respond to its controls.

There followed a hasty trek to examine the other platforms in the vicinity, but these were all similarly inactive; and thus the newcomers were sealed out on the surface while the para-ion men were sealed in the metal cavities below. The immediate suggestion was that they should use explosives to destroy one of the platforms and gain access to the shaft itself. It was Absolute who pointed out that they had not come equipped to handle a descent down a vertical well five kilometres deep. The final answer was to send for a space-engineering team from the orbiting war-force, who, with commendable speed and ingenuity managed to isolate the elevator from its former control circuitry and provide a new power in-feed from their own generators. This, however, took nearly an hour and during that time no word had been received from the men below ground; it was obvious that Absolute was becoming increasingly anxious about the time limits which had been programed into the modulator packs of the para-ion men.

Dam viewed this dislocation with suppressed glee, but knew it was no more than a preliminary matching of wits. Considering that the destructive capability of the Terrans represented an overkill potential of about a thousand times, it was obvious that while the defenders might introduce irritating delays there could be no doubt of the outcome—the occupants of Syman could not possibly win.

Absolute, who although nominally only a major,

carried an extra authority which easily outranked the more senior officers involved. She decided the next move immediately. She and Dam, in para-ion identity, would descend by the liberated elevator while a second platform would be similarly secured for use by the regular commandos. Her reasoning was simple: the first elevator to descend was bound to meet a very hot reception, one which only those in para-ion identity would be able to survive. Once through, they would secure the base of the second elevator, so that the regular commandos could enter without walking into a prepared trap. In the meantime further commandos were ordered down from orbit to follow up on the advantage thus gained.

Apprehensively, Dam submitted to the para-ion transition and joined Absolute on the elevator platform. Between them they had a small arsenal of radiation weapons with which to meet the trap into which they were descending. It was here that Dam was forced to marvel at Absolute's confidence and courage, and her firm conviction that the two of them alone could swing the battle and save the para-ion team from whatever it had become involved in. He could see though that two trained para-ion fighters could be worth more than a whole regiment of conventional commandos in such a situation. This point was viciously underscored when an elevator platform that had not been under direct observation unobtrusively descended and then returned to the surface bearing a blast bomb that killed most of the commandos already on the surface.

Recovering from the shock, the remaining men rallied to the all-important task of speeding the 'liberated' elevator on its way, bearing the indomitable

Absolute and the extremely apprehensive Dam. During the descent down the great polished-metal shaft Dam studied Absolute, wondering if she was similarly affected, but her face showed only the light of her dominating and unspoken passion, and, curiously, a hint of triumph.

Reluctantly, Dam began to marshal his weapons, knowing that regardless of his sympathies, his only route to personal survival lay in fighting his way through whatever waited at the foot of the shaft. It was certain that Absolute herself would kill him if he faltered for an instant in furthering her bloody cause. It was not that he valued his own life so highly as the fact that, knowing what he knew and being possessed now of inbuilt para-ion capability, his future potential for damaging Terra's aims depended on his being able to live to bear his knowledge back to the Hub. If maintenance of life meant killing a few allies now, it was a misfortune that must be balanced against greater final good. Even so, the idea tasted utterly bitter on his tongue, and his sole consolation was the comforting weight of the stolen pulse-activator that resided snugly in the pouch of his coverall.

CHAPTER XXI

One of the more remarkable pieces of technology to come out of the Hub was the development of the sling nets, by means of which hundred tonne slabs of rough-cut nickel iron could be captured out of orbit around Syman and accelerated to a tenth of the speed of light and sent on a precise trajectory for a twenty-year flight through space. No steel could stand the tensile stresses of the space sling; a clever composite had been devised. At the centre of each strand was a fine filament of metal so highly compressed that its atoms had been broken up and its component electrons and nuclei jammed together into a state of matter nearly as dense as that of white dwarfs. Around this incredible thread, no piece of which had ever been known to break and which alone contributed ninety eight percent of the net's weight, had been drawn a sheath of space-alloy able to stand the attrition and the stresses of the job even in the coldness of space. Many strands of the composite had been twisted together to make cable, and from the cable was woven the great nets which constituted the cosmic slings. On Syman, sling nets were plentiful.

THE ION WAR

Having gained control of one of the elevator platforms, the para-ion squad had descended two kilometres to the first level and emerged through the air-locks without meeting overt opposition. They found themselves in a broad metal gallery whose railed floor showed the means by which the blocks of nickel iron from the planet's interior were transported to the elevator platforms. The gallery was empty, and even though it was brightly lit it was doubtful if the para-ion men thought to question the significance of the sling net covering the high ceiling. Certainly they saw no danger in their immediate situation, as, with weapons readied, they advanced as an orderly group to menace the bright metal tunnels leading from the gallery. They were approximately half way to their first objective when the explosive bolts which retained the great sling net to the ceiling were fired simultaneously, and the heavy metal mesh fell down to cover them.

Such was the gross weight of the net that had the men not been in para-ion state the device would have crushed them instantly. The plasticity provided by the energy shells in which each identity was encapsulated ensured that most of them survived even though they were pinned helplessly to the ground by the hideous weight. Their agonies were real, however, due to the distortion of their energy shells, and the pain would not relent until the pressures were released.

Suddenly the gallery was flooded with sound as a voice spoke to them in a slow voice amplified as if to ape the last trumpet.

"Ion warriors, we give you a simple choice. Each of you is programed for destructive reversion if you

174

do not report for paraforming back to your normal
identity within the set time. We are quite prepared to
leave you where you are until this destructive reversion takes place, you understand?''

A silence had fallen over the trapped men as they
listened for whatever might follow.

''But there's a second way. Most of you are Hub
colonials impressed into Terran service. These we
are prepared to save, using our own paraformer. The
price is that those we take agree to dedicate themselves to Liam's war rather than Terra's. Whoever
wishes to co-operate will please try to make some
kind of sign.''

Among the severly distorted men on the floor
there was an immediate response, with a volley of
limbs waving through the mesh. Only the officer
commanding the squad showed any dissent. With a
superhuman effort he managed to adjust his position
and began to use a heavy-duty laser both to cut down
some of the loudspeakers and to attack the fabric of
the net which confined him.

Into the gallery from the side tunnels came half a
dozen strangely clad men also in para-ion identity,
with modulator packs of obviously improvised design. The officer turned his laser on them, but pre-
dictably without effect, and they walked towards
him. Each bore a large brick of rough-cut nickel
iron—when these were dropped upon him all his
movements ceased.

The strange ion-men explored the netted heap,
extricated weapons through the mesh, then brought
out a series of hoists with which they began to lift the
net from one end and slowly to recover the trapped
men. Dragging those whose energy shells were slow

in returning to the original configuration, they cleared the men onto little automatic trolleys which then sped away down the tunnels towards transformation back to molecular identity, and a swift and gruelling appraisal by Liam Liam.

Only the officer, still under a pile of metal bricks, remained when the warning signals indicated that the elevator platform was again on its way down from the surface. Forgetting their previous occupation, the strange para-ion men hastily took positions around the elevator air-lock in order that they could cover the area with their weapons. Having accounted for all members of the Terran para-ion team, it was a reasonable assumption that this time the platform would be bringing only conventional commandos. Liam's ion-men began firing even before the airlock seals were broken, and continued up to the point where they realized that the two figures who emerged unscathed through the blistering radiation-fire were para-ion people of a very different class.

The first figure was that of a woman who moved with a speed and proficiency thought to be impossible in the para-ion form. She literally leaped straight into a group of ghost defenders, scattering them physically, opposing their unnatural clumsiness with such a practised and vicious expertise that they fell back in consternation. Her companion, while not propelled with the same deadly enthusiasm, took an equally forbidding stance; after two minutes the newcomers controlled the field. Baffled, Liam's ion men retreated into the corridors, while the unbelievable ghost-woman, her face glowing with triumphant contempt, strode down the middle of the gallery and called out in a loud, clear voice.

"Liam Liam?"

"I hear you, you understand?" Liam's voice came back over the loudspeakers, but this time it was shorn of its former omnipotent overtones.

"Show yourself. We have to speak."

There was a pause, during which time nothing appeared to happen, then against the bright walls at the entrance of one of the tunnels Liam Liam appeared, the random reflections highlighting the intelligent ugliness of his features.

"You should not have come here," said Absolute directly. "You played your hand too soon, and in the wrong place. The whole purpose of the Syman encounter was to discover if you'd obtained para-ion capability—and if so, to destroy it. The fleet is waiting for only one piece of evidence that you've achieved what you have, then they'll stand-off and turn Syman into a sun. Nothing will escape."

"What would you have me do?"

"If Syman is surrendered totally and without resistance, perhaps the planet might be saved. But your ion-crew is a direct threat to any peaceful settlement. If Syman is not to be destroyed, there must be proof that your threat has been neutralized."

"What degree of proof would be acceptable?"

"Your heads would do. You could get all your men back into molecular identity and fetch them here. I will personally perform their execution. Or . . ."

"Or what?"

"If you have a ship, you can attempt to take it back into space. With what the fleet has waiting for you, there's scant chance of your making it alive,

177

but at least your danger will be transferred away from the planet itself.''

"Will that ensure the safety of Syman?"

"No. It will merely affect the probabilities. But it would be the only positive factor in the whole chain of decision.''

"Then I have little choice, you understand?'' A scurry of alarm signals indicated that a second platform had begun to leave the surface. ''But it will take a little time for me to get the vessel back into the elevator.''

"If time is all you need,'' said Absolute, ''then I may be able to find it for you.''

Liam saluted gravely, and ran back down the tunnel through which he had appeared. Absolute scanned the alarm signals and gained her bearings, selecting a route to the base of the elevator which was descending. Dam followed her, and she placed him precisely in front of the lock from which the commando squad was due to emerge.

"You know what to do, Lover?''

"Cover them,'' said Dam.

"No, you bloody fool! Kill them!''

"Kill . . .?''

"How the hell else can Liam Liam find the time to kick his ship off-planet? If these commandos get through, there'll be a running battle to the death. And when Command learns of the presence of a paraforming device down here they'll have no option but to turn Syman into a nova—and you and I will be components of it. Don't think they'll bother to clear out their own people first. We're strictly expendable.''

Dam selected his weapons gravely, and practiced

covering the lock entry with a wide sweep. At his side stood Absolute, weapon rested but as alert as a hunting animal, waiting for the air-lock to cycle. As the great doors opened a blistering hail of weapon fire swept out as the commandos, not knowing what kind of reception awaited them, attempted to secure their safe emergence. They were unlucky. Unscathed by the Terran weapons, Dam and Absolute opened fire. Soon the space was filled with a tangle of dead and twisted bodies. Dam and Absolute had to clear the dead limbs from the doors before they could close the lock and gain the elevator in an attempt to secure their own salvation in space via the pinnace they had left on the surface.

Liam Liam's ship was already under power as the elevator drove swiftly upwards. Even as the platform reached the surface, the little paraformer ship was clawing towards the heavens in a desperate attempt to pierce the net of vengeful spacecraft ranged above it.

The Terran fleet, however, was having its own problems. First had come the order to stand-off away from Syman in case it became necessary to drive the metal world into a nova. No sooner had the fleet started to manoeuvre than the space approaches had seemingly become filled with great hundred-ton masses of flying metal; the sling-ships of Syman had been joined by those from Toroliver in a concerted attempt to intercept and return to the vicinity of Syman's orbit a considerable proportion of the material distributed in recent months by the sling shuttle.

While the shielded cruisers were in very little direct danger from the inert slabs of flying metal, the presence of the objects monopolized the detectors and automatic gunnery circuits, and the fragmentation of the slabs when blown apart by missiles increased rather than decreased the navigational hazards and the incidence of alarms. Faced with the inability to maintain safe parking orbits in the vicinity of millions of tons of large nickel-iron shrapnel moving at every conceivable velocity and angle the sector commander ordered a retreat to a designated rendezvous in space.

As the warforce withdrew, the sector commander took the decision to eliminate Syman from space entirely. Two hellships dived to seed their cargoes: contra-charmed nuclei to catalyse a nuclear reaction that ran directly opposite to the normal evolution of heavy materials from elementary hydrogen. One hellship mishandled the time delay on the charge; both vessels were swallowed by the great, expanding ball of a miniature sun, newly created, which sprang into being where the metal world of Syman had previously had existence.

Taking advantage of the fleet's divided attention, the little paraformer ship bearing Liam Liam, his original crew and a full squad of Terran-trained para-ion men, streaked at suicidal speed through the litter of space debris, frenetically attempting to stay ahead of the leaping tongues of the infant sun. With a wary eye on the integrity of the radiation shields, which alone saved the ship from biological sterilization, Liam maintained a deadly calm. Those around him were still dumbfounded by the shock of Syman's wanton destruction, but Liam had already accepted the planet's loss as one of the graver sacrifices of the war. What the Syman incident had given him was sufficient experienced para-ion men to train an entire army if required; in this critical field he could soon achieve parity with Terra. Added to his previous grimness now was hope.

CHAPTER XXII

Absolute's objective, once they had gained the pinnace, had been to make for the mother-ship with all possible speed. As they had raced towards their objective she had been summoned to the radio to answer the sector commander's questions, and it was no great surprise to Dam when the stand-off order had come through shortly after they had gained the carrier.

Having lost all his para-ion companions, Dam now found himself in a class apart, with no flight or battle duties to perform. He took the opportunity to go to the navigation deck, from which point of vantage he could satisfy his curiosity about the outcome of the Syman campaign. The navigational crew paid him no attention, being fully occupied with the complex chore of manoeuvering safely to stand-off orbit in close proximity to the rest of the fleet. The operation was rendered even more hazardous by the inexplicable arrival of a great shower of metallic space-debris, surging through the space approaches, and which completely occupied the automatic alarm and gunnery systems. While the debris itself constituted only a minor hazard, the overshoot of the meteor-destruction gunnery among so many ships in close concentration added a dimension of risk which was not acceptable in a purely routine situation, and was logically followed soon after by an order to re-group at a rendezvous point well out in space.

Absolute had also come down to the navigation deck to observe the progress of the encounter, and Dam had taken to watching her nearly as closely as he was watching the screens portraying the activity out in space. Something about her exchange with the man called Liam Liam had caught his interest. He had the curious feeling that the two of them had met before, and that her subsequent action of allowing Liam to escape was something more than a ploy to secure her own salvation.

The screens were now cluttered with the multiple activities in progress, and it was not easy to follow the details properly, but his own battle-trained estimation was that in the confusion Liam Liam's little ship had managed to escape. If Absolute was following the same events as closely as he, she could scarcely have failed to come to the same conclusion but no hint of this showed in her face. Instead she appeared to be waiting with a trace of apprehension for what might follow.

The factor which brought both anger and relief to the margins of her eyes was the brilliant sunflare when Syman went nova. As the screens darkened protectively she rose to her feet as though the entire episode was ended, and walked straight past Dam without seeming to notice him. Although Dam's attention was engaged by the violence of the spectacle outside, the impression he caught of the will to destruct came not from the angry screens but from a sudden interpretation of the passion which inhabited Absolute. He remembered suddenly the group of dead Terran commandos which they had shot down at the foot of the elevator, and knew exactly why she had shown relief at Syman's destruction. Absolute had enabled Liam Liam and a whole para-ion squad to escape, and the death of Syman had obliterated both all the evidence of that and of the subsequent slaughter of the molecular form soldiers. Somehow it had not occurred to Dam before that his fate too had vested on the destruction of Syman. He could not however pinpoint why the event had made her angry.

Without a para-ion crew, the remaining paraforming ship in the craft-lock was useless, and the mother-ship would be nothing but a liability to the rest of the fleet in whatever action they were now to be assigned. After briefly touching the rendezvous point the mother-ship was ordered back to Terra, and this time the large escort craft was not provided. The result of this was that Absolute had no companion ship on which to travel, as she had on the outwards journey, and was quartered on the carrier itself.

Seeking to dig more deeply into the enigma of Absolute's role on Syman, Dam began studying her whenever possible, and attempting at all times to have a knowledge of her whereabouts. His purpose in this was not too clear except that there were a lot of unresolved questions to which she apparently held the key; and he was hoping that by word, deed or implication, a little piece more of the puzzle would fall into place.

Despite his vigilance, the answers actually came in an unexpected and potentially dangerous way, and arose in one of the situations where he had misjudged her intended movements. Taking advantage of his leisure, he had begun to explore the remaining para-former ship in the craft-lock, striving to familiarize himself with the mechanisms so thoroughly that he could rebuild one for the Hub if the opportunity ever presented itself. While he had the theory of paraforming clear in his mind, he was ignorant of many of the vital engineering details. To this end he had inched himself full length into a narrow space on top of the squared helices of the paraforming unit to examine the detail of some of the connections. As he was drawing himself over the uneven surface, how-ever, Absolute entered unexpectedly through the lock of the ship, and, unaware of his presence, made her way to the cupboard from which he had stolen the radio pulse activator.

Frozen in position, his breath consciously stilled, hoping his heartbeats were not as apparent to her as they were to himself, Dam waited, uncomfortable and anxious. He was painfully situated, and in at-tempting to ease himself he drew back slightly—and the accident happened. The pulse unit which was in his coverall pocket was dislodged by a turn of the coil on which he lay and fell through the helix, to clatter loudly on to the deck below.

Whether she actually saw the object fall was a matter of conjecture, but she picked it up with quick alarm, glanced speculatively towards the cupboard from which it had been taken, and wheeled round, electron pistol in hand.

"Come out, whoever you are! Else I burn you where you lay." From her positioning it was obvious that she had deduced exactly where Dam was hid-den.

"Don't shoot, Absolute! I'm coming down."

"Lover!" The relief in her voice was as surprising

as it was emphatic, and the electron pistol was lowered. "Get the hell out of there!"

Dam wormed his way out from the top of the coil and dropped back to the floor. "Absolute, I . . ."

"You'd better hang on to this, Lover." With a swift movement of her hands she returned the pulse unit to him. "The way things are going we'll be needing all the advantage we can muster."

"We?" He suspected she was tormenting him, but there was no sign of mockery in her face. "You mean . . .?"

"I mean time's running out for the both of us. The sector commander can't *prove* what happened on Syman, but he's highly suspicious. Fortunately he isn't familiar with the details of para-forming, he doesn't know about the pulse units. I'm under open arrest until the ship makes planetfall on Terra, and you're to be held as a witness. Knowing their method of interrogation, we've only one option open to us."

"What's that?"

"Escape. The first instant this ship makes contact with anything, anywhere, we adopt para-ion form and attempt to fight our way out. Better to go down fighting than be taken for questioning."

In a dizzying cascade the pieces of the puzzle tumbled together in Dam's mind, opening vistas more fascinating than any he had dared hope to find. He found himself toying wildly with the idea that Absolute herself was from the Hub, a notion which suddenly explained the way only colonials had managed to survive her training regime, and why she had admonished Liam Liam for playing his hand too soon and in the wrong place. He felt impelled to ask the question.

"Are you a colonial, too?"

THE ION WAR

"From Castalia, like yourself. Why else do you think you were sent to help me?"

"Sent . . .?" Dam traced his way through the threads of circumstance that had placed him in this situation—and emerged still baffled.

"You were hand-picked for this project, Lover. Almost reared for it, I'd say. Guess father hasn't lost his touch in judging men."

"Who is your father?"

"Senator Anrouse. Do you know him?"

"I've met him but once, though I'm told he had a great influence on my career."

"The old fox sitting in the background pulling strings. He's a very dedicated man."

"He'd need to be to allow his daughter to do what you've been doing."

There was the sudden sound of someone opening the doors of the craft lock, and the noise of heavy football moving down the catwalks to the paraformer craft on the ramp. Absolute searched wildly.

"They're already too suspicious. They mustn't find me here." She was looking for a place in which to hide, but there was no possible point of concealment except for the top of the paraforming coils, and no time for her to insinuate herself into the narrow recess from which Dam had emerged.

Dam came to a sudden decision. "If we can't conceal your location, at least we can disguise the interest."

"What . . .?"

By way of answer he scooped her up in a long, passionate, embrace, to which, after her initial surprise, she yielded with an enthusiasm not entirely the product of the urgency of the situation. Behind Dam the door-lock opened and the footsteps entered, faltered, then retreated, betraying a slight buoyancy, as if the walker was amused. By now Dam was again conscious of the slight texture of the metal mesh beneath her flesh, but this time it added a piquancy which heightened rather than repelled his interest. They were manifestly two of a kind, and already shared a bond more common than most couples could know. It was a long time before the communion was finally broken.

"Who was that who came in?" asked Dam at last.

"Dug Rette, ship's security officer. He's the one responsible for handing me over to the authorities on Terra."

"Did we fool him?"

"We weren't fooling anyone, Lover. That was for real! When I chose your call-name, I was smarter than I knew."

"Speaking of call names, what's your own name, Absolute?"

"You'll not believe this, but Absolute Anrouse was what I was christened." She re-buttoned her tunic and turned away with new purpose, heading towards the cupboard in which the pulse units were stored. Taking one out, she examined it, then gave her head a quick shake of alarm.

"What's the matter?" Dam asked.

She pointed to a detail on the instrument too small for Dam to be able to discern from a distance, then pressed a test button and waited for the tell-tale to glow. It remained dark. With speculative agitation, she operated the paraforming control itself, and waited with anxious breath. The hoped-for transformation into the para-ion state did not occur. With a rising tide of concern she flung the pulse unit back into the cupboard, and selected another and then another as each one failed.

"The bastards!" Her face was full of angry shock. "They've anticipated us. Sabotaged the whole damn lot."

"Mine still works," said Dam. "At least, it did."

"When did you take it?"

"Well before we went down on Syman."

"That's it then! The units we actually used on Syman, and all the remaining spares, have since been tampered with. The one they missed was the one you'd already taken."

"Can't it be used for both of us?"

"Not without a major re-wire. They're specifically tuned to the modulator implants."

"Does that mean we can't fight our way out?"

"I can't. You must. For God's sake you've to make the best of any break you can get."

"Even if it means leaving you behind?"

"Lover, if I can't escape, your remaining alongside isn't going to do any good for either of us. You've to try and make it back to Liam Liam. Show him what the next phase of para-ion warfare is liable to be like, because his old tactics won't stand a snowflake's chance in hell. You carry the future of the Hub underneath your skin. Whatever it costs, get back to the Hub alive."

"I don't see why we didn't go with Liam Liam when we met on Syman," said Dam bitterly.

"There was no way. If we'd not been there to stop those commandos in the shaft, not even Liam could have got away. We'd all be making our tiny contribution to that nova. It's that sort of a bloody war."

CHAPTER XXIII

The exercise during the Lightning campaign in which Liam's communications ship had been inserted in the Terran FTL radio link had been useful in many ways. One advantage had been the on-line computer access to the message codes, from which a great deal of cipher information had been extracted. Although now remaining in a passive role out in deep-space, the same ship was still engaged in monitoring Terran operational transmissions, and feeding the pith of this intelligence back to base and to the radio-room of the *Starbucket*.

It was information gained in this way which creased Liam's brow when he finally rejoined his old vessel. From the sector commander responsible for the campaign against Syman had gone a series of messages to Terran Intelligence questioning the integrity of a Major Absolute of Para-ion Technological Operations. The replies were not encouraging. Her superior, code-named Abel, had apparently long been suspicious of her motivation, and the final instruction was to arrange for her arrest and interrogation.

The fate of a single individual was not normally

something to cause Liam Liam very much concern: the sacrifices of war had already involved the loss of whole planets and populations—but the value of the information which this one individual was known to carry made her of the greatest tactical importance. Having no light cruisers available, Liam decided that the *Starbucket* itself should shadow the mother ship as it sped on its way towards Terra. This could only safely be achieved from a distance which lay at the extreme end of their instrument range, and the venture became further complicated and hazardous when they entered the regions dominated by the great Terran ship chains.

The *Starbucket* passed the first chain without detection, but its second encounter could conceivably have been fatal. They had entered unknowingly inside the weapon-range of a large man-of-war which had been keeping careful station shielded against detection by the radiation barrage of a particularly vociferous sun. Before the *Starbucket* had time to turn and run, the man-of-war had detected the little ship's coming and was engaged in carving a furious intercept course. Once clear of the radio emanations from the sun it began demanding the newcomer's identity. Euken Tor bravely used his knowledge of Terran identification codes in an attempt to talk their way through; but the bluff failed, and for a few tense moments it looked as though an armed showdown was inevitable.

Warily, Liam summed the size and armaments of their massive opponent. He decided that the *Starbucket*'s special weaponry was probably capable of taking the man-of-war out of space. However, the removal of one ship could only trigger the rest of the chain into action, and there was no way the little ship could protect itself against a battlefleet. Their sudden hope of salvation came from something else he noticed as the vengeful ship swum in front of his high-resolution scanner—and that was the coloured pennant-bands on the front antenna. To the amazement of his deck officers, Liam flung out a sudden oath and raced for the communications handset.

"*Calendaria* ahoy! You're a tithe-loan vessel out of Ross unless I miss my guess. We're also from the Hub."

"What of it?" The answering voice sounded harsh and metallic over the speakers.

"This is the *Starbucket*—an action-ship of Liam's war, on a mission of importance to all our futures, you understand?"

Everyone on the *Starbucket*'s bridge who heard the message flinched visibly, and waited for the space-barrage to open up. The master-gunner's knuckles showed white as they gripped the safety trigger of his weapon controls. There was a long period of agonized silence, then a different voice came through on the radio.

"Greetings, Liam Liam! It's a dangerous game you play."

"Not more dangerous than living on one of Terra's target worlds, you understand?"

"Point taken! We didn't see you come or go. Keep your data-links open, and we'll try to give you headings to avoid the rest of the local ship chains. Bon voyage!"

As the *Starbucket*'s engines strained to regain their lost velocity, Euken Tor mopped his brow.

"You took one hell of a gamble there, Liam! That

ship could easily have had a Terran crew, or at least a Terran master.''

''Then I promise you we'd not have gone out of space alone. But believe me, a Terran commander always had his own colour bands on the antenna. It's a matter of prestige, you understand?''

Liam was now concentrating on the fleeting traces at the extreme edge of the scanning range, which was all the evidence they had about the passage of the paraformer mother-ship. Urging the last ounce of resolution from the scanner, he noted with some satisfaction that the carrier's course was being diverted to take it through one of the permitted movement channels. Liam estimated that if he could take advantage of the diversion and manage to carve a straight course through the waiting patrols, they had a good chance of achieving a position from which to operate the daring plan forming in his mind.

Euken Tor whistled incredulously at the proposal, then, seeing the look on Liam's face, gave instructions for the necessary preparations. He himself analyzed the data-link information supplied by the *Calendaria*, and used it to map out a projected tachyon-space trajectory which held only a statistically small chance of their being intercepted by the random Terran patrols.

Liam Liam became busy in other ways. He was studying a manual of space-traffic regulations, signal responses, and orbital transfer routines relating to the Solar system, whilst at the same time repolishing both the style and the brass stars of a supposed sector commander called Mail, whose whereabouts had been the subject of much conjecture since the end of the Lightning campaign. With the laws of probability aided by many impious prayers and a minimum-radiation mode of flight, the little *Starbucket* seemed to have a charmed existence, as it picked its way through the remainder of the ship-chains without challenge, and incredibly avoided even the random scans of the tachyon-space patrols. Then, slightly amazed by their own audacity, they found themselves suddenly amidst the bewildering cluster of spacecraft on the fringes of the Solar system itself.

It was a piece of sheer bravado which merited its own reward. Had it been detected inflight in a deep-space location, the presence of the *Starbucket* would have raised instant suspicion and challenge: its apparently casual and innocent insertion into the circulating ships awaiting permission to enter the Solar transfer orbits, however, provoked no such concern. Euken Tor made the customary responses to the Solar Traffic control, claiming the ship was on an Intelligence liaison mission, and was automatically granted permission to remain in an outer station. Since they had not signalled a request to enter the transfer orbits, Euken was taking a gamble that their claimed identity would not be processed through the usual data channels and its bogus nature deduced by the refusal of some destination port to accept a request for planetfall.

Nonetheless, their position still contained the very real danger that some other information network was already striving to match their identity against an entry on authorized shipping lists, and when no match was found there would arise the inevitable string of queries. Failure to find satisfactory answers to a further interrogation would invite the attention of armed patrol ships and the near-certainty of being destroyed by the immense fire-power which could be brought to bear in their direction. Euken Tor sat at his control desk on the *Starbucket*'s bridge and sweated, whilst Liam Liam scanned the space approaches for the first signs of the coming of the paraformer carrier which he intended to intercept. They estimated they had beaten the mother ship to its destination by about eighteen hours—which was a small margin by space travel standards, but a long time to sit under Terran guns while high-speed data processing and instant communications might at any moment reveal the clandestine nature of their presence. As Euken said, they were stretching the upper limit of their luck to its upper limit.

As it happened, the challenge to their identification codes and the sighting of the mother-ship were almost simultaneous. Euken contrived to keep the situation confused by re-issuing his original answers with a few of their figures transposed, while at the same time bringing the *Starbucket* round to match trajectories with the approaching ship. By the time the revised identity signals had been rejected, the *Starbucket* was well out of the traffic lanes and had the mother-ship clear on its screens.

Liam Liam, in the pose of Security Commander Mail, was already speaking dictatorially over the radio to the ship's captain and its security officer.

"This order overrides those you've previously received, you understand? Prepare yourself for boarding, and have the prisoner known as Absolute available for transfer to my custody."

"I still insist that we have not received the requisite clearance." The carrier captain's voice sounded extremely unhappy.

"Clearance!" Liam's voice worked itself up to a passable imitation of incensed megalomania. "I decide what clearances are issued and to whom. I'd advise you not to throw bureaucratic obstruction in my way, Captain, else I can make life very uncomfortable for you, you understand?"

"I understand." The captain's voice sounded suitably subdued. "We are preparing to receive your boarding party. Please proceed in your own time."

Liam Liam would have preferred to have taken the majority of his ship's company and stormed the carrier, but the *Starbucket*'s little pinnace could accommodate nine people at most, and thus he had to be content with six shipmen dressed in Terran service coveralls, ostensibly to serve as an armed escort for the prisoner. While he had hopes that bluff would suffice he knew that he must be prepared to fight his way out if necessary. Thus, in addition, to their obvious arms, each of his men was provided with a number of concealed weapons, including sufficient knock-out gas to overwhelm the entire crew of the carrier. Several open radio links with the *Starbucket* were arranged so that a listening watch could be established and a rescue operation mounted if things went wrong.

As the pinnace approached the space transfer hatch of the mother-ship, Security Commander Mail thrust his way impatiently through the opening space-lock to meet the captain and officers who were awaiting his entry. The woman called Absolute had been held handcuffed and in leg irons in a cell, and was now being brought down a corridor by armed crewmen. Her look of recognition on seeing Liam was instantly quenched as she realized the nature of the deception he was playing, but although she did not speak, Liam could sense a great deal of genuine unease in her manner. Where he should have read quiet hope in her eyes, he read instead the imminence of an uncertain catastrophe.

By means of a pre-arranged hand signal, Liam brought to his escort an awareness that something was amiss, and a secret codeword over the open radio link similarly alerted the crew of the *Starbucket*. Meanwhile Liam, who could yet detect no cause for alarm save for the suppressed distress in Absolute's expression, was concerning himself with browbeating the captain and his security officer in a manner he imagined was in the best traditions of the Terran Security Service. He was on the point of securing an abject apology when a sudden disturbance broke out somewhere on the ship, and the whipcrack of an electron pistol on full beam echoed loud through the corridors.

Inexplicably, the mother-ship's captain and his officers seemed as perplexed as was Liam, and some of the officers hurried off to investigate. The object of their concern, however, was already running towards them in the shape of a lone warrior in para-ion state, intent on killing anyone who threatened to stand between him and the space-lock. Liam recognized the figure as being the one who had been Absolute's companion on Syman. Unfortunately, being pinned down as he was by electron fire, there was no way in which Liam could communicate his good intentions. Instead, one of Liam's men, with a tactical mistake pardonable in the heat of the moment, attempted to stop the approaching runner with a knockout gas capsule. The gas had no effect at all on the para-ion figure, but everyone else was.

As Liam fought against the tide of blackness he saw the para-ion warrior stop before the form of the unconscious Absolute and attempt to drag her towards the space-lock. Far down a corridor behind him, and as yet unaffected by the gas, one of the mother-ship's officers opened fire with an electron carbine, the fire from which seriously endangered everyone on the deck and threatened to render the door of the space-lock inoperable. Seeing this latter possibility, the para-ion figure reluctantly abandoned his attempt to carry Absolute with him, and fled into the lock, closing it behind him. Then, with his last thread of consciousness departing, Liam heard the engines of the *Starbucket*'s pinnace strike a mighty reactive blow against the carrier's hull as the minute craft and its lone occupant departed into space.

CHAPTER XXIV

Although he had been prepared to fight Dam found the pinnace unoccupied and its engines already primed, as though a fast departure had been intended. This circumstance greatly speeded him on his way. Dropping back from his para-ion to normal molecular identity, he seized the controls and gunned the little vessel away from the great hull of the carrier. He immediately came under fire from another vessel close-by, and found the only escape route open to him was to manoeuvre the pinnace in a tight turn that brought the carrier's bulk between himself and the guns being deployed against him. Then, carefully aligning his craft to remain behind the carrier's shielding mass, he turned the pinnace again, and headed straight out into space.

The success of this escape method did not promise to be great. He expected, each second, to be taken out of space by some well directed fire of larger calibre, but for some reason the attack was not continued, and he soon had put a useful distance between himself and the two ships. It was only then that he had the opportunity to try and analyze what had taken place. He had expected a senior security officer to come aboard to take possession of himself and Absolute—he had based his escape plan on it. What he had not planned on was the gas capsule. The point worried him: an escort shipman having the authority to use one was absolutely contrary to what he knew of Terran military discipline. Something about the whole episode was terribly wrong.

His suspicions were increased by the pinnace itself: the controls had come so automatically to his hands that in the anxiety of his flight he had not noticed that the instrument boards were laid out according to accepted Hub conventions, not those of the mother planet. With the awful idea dawning on him that he might have foiled a Hub espionage operation he turned in alarm to the scanners to review the situation he had left behind. Any thoughts he might have had of returning to the mystery ship which had intercepted the carrier were instantly destroyed: the vessel was already making remarkable progress towards tachyon-space entry-velocity.

The reason for the mystery ship's hasty departure became immediately obvious—and was also a threat to Dam's own safety: three Terran corvettes of the Solar Patrol were streaking towards the fleeing vessel. Whether or not they caught it before it could enter tachyon space it was certain that very soon they would turn their attentions to the pinnace. Dam watched with stilled breath, willing them to maintain their present course, which was at right-angles to his own; if they did so for a sufficient length of time he might drop out of scanner range. The pinnace would be very difficult to re-locate once lost.

He began to turn his attention to the pinnace itself. He soon realized that he was in possession of no ordinary craft. The vessel had no armaments, yet despite its diminutive size it was beautifully equipped, its facilities even including a limited tachyon space capability with energy reserves sufficient for a couple of average jump phases. What it lacked was a computing facility sufficient to calculate drop-out point of such a jump. It was a facility which could not have been included in such a small craft, and presumably the jump calculations were normally supplied by data transfer-link from the pinnace's parent ship. The point prompted Dam to try the data-link in the vague hope that the connection was still functioning, but the display showed nothing but the random static of Sol's own broadcast radiation.

In the moment of agonized indecision during the escape from the carrier he had obeyed Absolute's precept that one of them must escape even if it meant leaving the other to perish or remain in captivity. Dam knew that the onus was very much upon him to reach the Hub with all possible speed in order to warn the resistance movement of Terra's breakthrough in para-ion techniques. Against the need for speed, however, had to be set the necessity of avoiding capture or destruction by the Terrans, else the sacrifice of Absolute would have been wasted. For this reason Dam was forced to think the unthinkable, to consider, if the need arose, taking a blind leap through tachyon space simply to escape the Terran ships behind him. It was a desperate last resort measure, and one he fervently hoped would not become necessary.

Events, however, took the decision out of his hands. At the very last moment before it would have gone beyond scanning range, one of the Terran corvettes peeled away from its companion ships and turned in Dam's direction. Already possessed of superior velocity, and having engines a thousand times more powerful than those of the pinnace, it bore towards him like a dark angel, and there was no doubting its ability to overrun the little craft, nor uncertainty about the destructive nature of its mission. Dam watched aghast as the little flotilla of homing missiles speared ahead of the terrible avenger. The premature flare of one of the missles was his final warning: with no time to take even a rough heading towards the direction of the Hub, he threw the pinnace into a despairing leap into tachyon space for which no dropout point had been present.

It was a very rough entry. His craft had barely achieved entry velocity and his unfamiliarity with the miniature control panel as well as the lack of computer trimming had comspired to tunnel the ship through the light barrier at a very bad phase-angle. Fearfully, he felt the ship being caught in the grip of the elements of trans-relativity as the power meters swung sickeningly and the gallant little vessel fought to escape the daunting dead hand of Einsteinian physics and reach the universe beyond.

Then, by some miracle, the marvellous little pinnace was floating free in the theoretical infinity called tachyon space. In the large spacecraft in which Dam normally served, tachyon space conditions were regarded as a physical abstraction, and actual observations were rare. By contrast, the broad viewports of the pinnace afforded no chance to avoid the multiple paradoxes of light and shade which characterized the alter-universe in which he was immersed, and for the first time in his space career Dam experi-

THE ION WAR

enced the wonder and perplexity known to the early pioneers when they first penetrated the light barrier into the realms beyond.

Dam's main reaction was one of immediate relief, because for the moment he was relatively safe from attack. The corvette which had been pursuing him was unlikely to follow through into tachyon space, because few captains would dare to enter the region without a carefully pre-calculated dropout point. Furthermore, although there were Terran patrols actually operating within the tachyon domain, the restraints of trans-light physics were such that they were unable to alter speed to intercept without suffering severe penalties from time-dilation effects on their return to normal space. The most the tachyon patrols could do was to signal his position and probable drop-out co-ordinates to a normal-space patrol; they could not actively menace him while he remained in the inverse region.

Dam's respite, however, was short-lived; he found to his dismay that his power reserves had already fallen below the danger margin. This was a consequence of entering tachyon space with insufficient velocity; a similar energy penalty would be paid during the drop-out maneuver back to normal space. A quick calculation showed him that unless he dropped out of tachyon space immediately, he would return to normal space with virtually no motive power available. Although the communications and life-support systems had their own auxiliary power supplies, he would be stranded far from the ship lanes and without the capacity for even limited sub-light travel. Therefore, even though his tachyon flight had been of considerably less duration than he had considered safe, he flung the craft into the drop-out mode and waited anxiously to see just where he would arrive.

Immediately Dam had a dramatic example of one of the reasons why blind emergence from tachyon space was an occupation for fools and those smitten with a death-wish. He dropped not into unoccupied space, as he had expected, but into the centre of a massive concentration of warcraft in parking orbit around a planet he was reasonably certain was Venus. He broke into a cold sweat at the thought of what might have happened had his drop-out point actually been inside the planet's bulk, and he could have wept with frustration at finding that he had not fled the Solar System, but had actually penetrated more deeply into it!

There was, however, no time for emotional concerns. He had re-entered normal space with all of his original tachyon space entry velocity, and was plunging planetwards in a powered flight intensified by the planet's own gravitational attraction. He had to use virtually all the remains of his drive energy just to curve his course and bring him finally back to a safe orbital situation. Unfortunately this brought him too close to the massed fleet for his meteoric arrival to remain unnoticed. There he was forced to sit, with no further chance of escape, while inquisitive little lifecraft emerged from one of the warcraft to investigate this strange new arrival in their midst.

CHAPTER XXV

The first man to recover from the gas was the crewman who had thrown the capsule in a vain attempt to stop the para-ion warrior's charge. Realizing he had made a gross error, he had uscd his last instant of fading consciousness to insert filter tubes into his nostrils, thus receiving a minimum of exposure to the gas. His re-awakening had come only shortly after Dam's blast-off, and his first action on rewaking had been to treat Absolute and his comrades to similar filters, and to ensure their mouths were closed. Then he strove to summon assistance from the *Starbucket* over the radio link.

Euken Tor, in charge of the Z-ship, however, already had his own share of problems. He was under Liam's orders to avoid the *Starbucket*'s capture or destruction at all costs, and already streaking into weapon range were three of the deadly corvettes of the Solar Patrol. If Euken had had a second pinnace available he would certainly have attempted a rescue even at such a precariously late time, but he had already seen his sole pinnace jet rapidly behind the mother-ship's hull and known, sickly, that there was totally insufficient time to get a crew into space suits and make the crossing between the ships the hard way. He found himself with no alternative but to abandon Liam and his party and put the *Starbucket* into crash-flight to try and escape the corvettes.

Liam Liam woke up cursing, partly from the side effects of the knockout gas, and partly because he already knew the pinnace was lost. He struggled drunkenly to his feet just in time to hear Euken Tor's regretful signing-off over the radio link. His comprehension of the situation was immediate, and was swiftly followed by a shrewd assessment of what routes to survival still lay open to them. The members of the carrier's crew, including the captain and several officers, were still unconscious on the deck around him. Without the slightest trace of hesitation Liam drew his electron pistol and killed them all where they lay. Their deaths were a pointed reminder that the only advantage he possessed was the element of surprise, assuming he could get his own sleeping shipmen back into action fast enough.

Fortunately the insertion of filters into their nostrils had been sufficiently swift to isolate them from all but the initial dose, and the remainder of the gas was already being picked up by the ship's ventilation system. A few hard slaps across the face sufficed to awaken most of Liam's men swiftly, and even Absolute finally responded to a rough shaking.

"What the hell's happened?" she asked.

"Chaos, you understand? Your boyfriend took off with the pinnace, and Euken Tor has had to make a hasty retreat in the *Starbucket*. Our only chance is to seize control of this carrier. I want you in para-ion identity—fast."

"It can't be done, Liam!" She looked at him regretfully. "They sabotaged my control unit, else I'd probably have gone out through that lock with Lover. You and your damn disguises! Don't you know it's you he's gone looking for?"

"Later I shall explain why I do not ambush Terran ships using my own name. How many crew does this vessel carry?"

"About seventy men."

"That's only ten to one against; we've got a fighting chance. We have stun grenades and handfighting experience they probably don't possess." Liam released her bonds, took a spare electron pistol from his pocket, and thrust the weapon into her hands. "Whenever you see a Terran, shoot to kill. We can't afford prisoners, you understand?"

He called his men together for a quick conference, then they scattered hastily to take up firing positions. Incredibily, news of what had taken place around the space-lock had not yet been communicated to the rest of the ship, and so the precious advantage of surprise still remained on the attackers' side. Liam lobbed the first stun grenade down a main passage, and they all ducked back out of sight as the pico-pulse stung the air around them. Then they followed through fast, killing fallen men as they reached them, and having only a brief battle with the be-mused crewmen who had survived the initial blast. Soon the whole deck level was theirs.

On the second level they failed to stun more than a third of the attendant crew, but fortunately very few of the remainder had immediate access to weapons, and the confrontation was mercifully brief though untidy. Approaching the third and fourth levels they were more cautious, and had only unconscious men to dispose of. It was only on the fifth and last level that a serious resistance developed, but even this was finally overcome by the bloody-minded desperation of the Hub invaders.

Then suddenly the carnage was over and Liam's tired and sweating group found themselves in undisputed control of the whole mother-ship. Even before they attended to the bodies of their victims they had to get the carrier under way and well clear of the Solar system. All the men Liam had brought with him were highly trained shipmen, many of them former officers, and they expertly divided the ship-control chores between them, each racing to handle his assignment and each contriving to handle a job normally the task of several men.

Calling for Absolute to assist him, Liam headed for the bridge, and as soon as he was assured of the power and the handling ability he swung the carrier through a broad arc to bring it to a heading approximately towards the Hub. Then he gunned the engines to build up tachyon space entry velocity, and bent to the task of setting the course co-ordinates needed to take them into and out of the initial jumps. It was several hours later, when the first jump had been safely entered and most of the former crew had been heaved into the space-disposal chutes, that Linc Maalham called from the communications room.

"Liam, I've managed to establish contact with the *Starbucket*. They've escaped the Patrol and Euken wants to know where to make rendezvous."

"I've decided to stay on this ship. There are too many advantages in remaining aboard. There's a serviceable paraforming ship on the ramps below, and a second mother-ship will be more than useful when Wing Ai's building program starts producing. Tell Euken to head for base, we'll join him there. Have him arrange for Wing Ai's laboratories to be standing by to explore the latest developments in para-ion, which we're bringing with us. I think we've achieved the breakthrough we needed, you understand?''

''Understood, Chief! Message on its way.''

Despite the under-manning, the carrier continued successfully on its way. Occasional reference to the *Starbucket* gave them the co-ordinates to avoid the great ship-chains, and by the end of the seventh leap they were well within the Hub sector, soon to be home. Even while coping with the workload of four communications men, Linc Maalham had found time to apply his electronic talents to the repair of Absolute's paraforming pulse unit. The sabotage of the controls had been undertaken by somebody with no great technical knowledge, and the internal damage had been massive rather than selective. By utilizing pieces from all the spares, Linc had contrived to build one new unit from the undamaged parts, but he was working without circuit schematics or a full knowledge of the instrument's function. His eyes were doubtful as he brought it to Liam and Absolute for a test.

''We can't afford to lose you, you understand?'' said Liam to Absolute. ''What happens to you if Linc has his circuits incorrect?''

Absolute was speculative. ''A failure to transpose me into para-ion identity would only leave us precisely where we are. But if I make the transition and it fails to bring me out of it again, then we've really got problems.''

Liam was decisive. ''Then it's a risk we daren't

take. We'll have to let Wing Ai's lab check it out theoretically first.''

He broke off as Linc, summoned by an automatic alarm, doubled away to the communications room. He returned a few minutes later, nearly out of breath.

''Liam, an urgent message from *Starbucket*. Hub Intelligence reports a new punitive fleet heading out from Sol towards the Hub.''

''Destination?''

''They're not sure yet. The information hasn't been transmitted, so they're probably sailing under sealed orders. Intelligence is trying to get a series of triangulations on the fleet so they can calculate where it's heading. They suggest, from the number of ships involved, that they might be preparing to attack one of the major worlds. But here's the interesting bit—the Terran fleet has called for a follow-up of a paraformer carrier and para-ion crew to join them in orbit.''

''The Devil they have!'' Liam's face lit with a smile of ever increasing dimensions and ugliness. ''Get *Starbucket* to patch me a communications channel through to base, Linc. When that paraformer carrier hits space I want her eliminated —very quietly. As for the Terran warfleet, it will have a para-ion team, though not quite the one they were expecting. And make contact with Wing Ai. We've got to make rendezvous to bring our other paraforming ship on to the ramps here and get a full complement of men aboard. If even one ship of that fleet ever reaches home again it'll be because we haven't been trying, you understand?''

''Understand, Chief!''

Linc's attention was suddenly diverted to Absolute, who had reached across the desk and was holding the paraforming pulse control in her hand. He watched with fascination as she deliberately pressed the actuator button on the untested instrument. Her transition into para-ion identity was immediate, and she spun and leaped easily in front of the startled men in order to demonstrate the advantages and mobility of the new para-ion technique. Then followed the moment of truth. Her hand hesitated above the button as she considered the terrible predicament in which she had placed herself if the unit failed to work. She pressed—and a wave of relief possessed them all; her return to normality was as precise and immediate as her exit had been.

Liam Liam mopped his brow thankfully. "I appreciate why you did that, Absolute, but I'd already told you not to take the risk."

"Sorry, Liam, but I had to know if it still worked."

"Then let me explain—if you intend to work with me, there's a subject you've to learn to apply to yourself. It's called discipline, you understand?"

"I'm no stranger to discipline, Liam, believe me. But that was something we needed to know right now. If you're laying plans to take the Terran fleet apart, somebody with inbuilt para-ion ability might be the crucial key which makes sense of all the rest. And, so help me, those Terran bastards are long overdue for the thrashing of their lives! I should know. Neither inside or out is there any part of me which doesn't bear their scars."

CHAPTER XXVI

As he waited for the lifecraft to approach, Dam surveyed the assembled fleet, and realized suddenly the situation into which he had arrived. The line-up of ships was of a campaign fleet similar to that he had observed in action against Syman and to those reported to have been deployed against Rigon and Zino. Venus was obviously the assembly point for the task fleets which were sent on punitive expeditions to the 'dissident' Hub worlds, and to judge from the completeness of the array, this fleet, too, would soon be on its way.

The immediate consequence of this line of speculation was the realization that of all potential routes which might take him back to the Hub, this fleet itself represented the most direct method. While not being sure how his conveyance could be achieved, he found himself looking for ways in which he might use the great warfleet to aid him in the direction of his destination. If he allowed himself to be captured it could not help achieve his objective, because although he had para-ion capability built into his body, he was unlikely to be allowed to retain the pulse unit which activated it. He did not think he would have a reasonable chance of escape at the Hub end of the journey if he did not have access to his para-ion capabilities. The problem was therefore how to board one of the ships and retain his mobildity at the end of the trip.

His first idea was that he might adopt a para-ion identity and travel as a sort of ghostly stowaway. He rejected the idea firstly because he could think of no suitable location on a ship where he might remain undetected for the entire journey, and secondly because he had no idea how long he could safely maintain a para-ion state. An alternative notion of trying to bluff his way through as a member of the regular Service force seemed even less promising until he realized that he was already wearing an authentic Terran uniform, and strictly speaking was a legitimate member of a Terran fighting force. As a lifecraft grappled for the hatch he swiftly put together the elements of his story and came to a swift decision as to how it ought to be played. Then with the para-forming pulse unit in his pocket and a prayer on his lips he went to the lock to greet the boarding party.

"Security Assassin Stormdragon," he announced in response to the yet unspoken question. "I regret the untimely arrival, but other duties delayed me I feared the fleet might get under way without me if I waited transport by normal channels." He contrived to make his voice as nonchalant as possible.

The officer's face still showed an open question. "You must be aware that tachyon dropouts within the solar planetary approaches are strictly forbidden?"

". . . Except in cases of extreme emergency."
Dam found himself quoting from the texts of the
orbital transfer routines he had used on his first
arrival on the Castalian *Starspite*. "My emergency
was extreme. If you don't believe me, read the
reserve energy banks."

The officer read the gauges, and his eyes widened
appreciably. He must have been as aware as was
Dam that a space-crash had been averted by only the
narrowest of margins. "The Fleet Traffic Commander has ordered your arrest. You can explain
your reasons to him."

"Willingly, but he will have to wait. Who's heading Security this trip?"

"Sub-Sector Neilson."

"Then I must speak with him first. Take me there
immediately."

"I have my orders," said the officer, faintly
hesitant.

"Dammit!" Dam let simulated wrath explode in
his voice. "Do you think I took those risks to get
here just so that I could face a tete-a-tete with a fleet
traffic commander? Take me to Sub-Sector Neilson,
and if anyone else thinks they've a claim on my time
I'll accommodate them later."

"But . . ."

"Do you know the motto of the Assassins Service, Captain? 'The only thing forbidden is failure'.
Think on it, and get me to Neilson as fast as you're
able. If you delay me I'll raise a charge of obstruction against you."

The officer shrugged, and backed out through the
hatch into the lifecraft. Dam followed, uncomfortably aware that he had passed only the first of many

hurdles he would face on his journey back to the Hub.

Security Sub-Sector Neilson heard his story with an expression which gave no hint of his underlying feelings. Then he looked thoughtfully at the palms of his hands.

"I find all this most irregular," he said doubtfully.

"Assassination's irregular," said Dam. "But somebody has to stop Liam Liam before he brings the rest of the Hub together. The job's been given to me, since the fleets have proved incapable of the task."

"Surely I should have had official notice of your coming?"

"Then you underestimate the reach of Hub Intelligence. Had that notice gone out on transmission, Liam Liam would certainly have been forewarned."

"But papers, even . . ."

"What use is an espionage assassin who carries papers? No, Sub-Sector, the only way to ensure complete security for the operation was to tell nobody in advance, and for me to reveal my status only to those who need to know. That's why I came direct to you."

"But suppose you aren't who you say you are at all?" This was a rhetorical rather than an actual question, yet Dam sensed a diamond hardness behind Neilson's attitude.

"Hell! Would you ask an assassin to prove his ability to kill? And what sort of demonstration would satisfy you?"

"One sufficient to justify a hyper-security rating."

"You'd be a brave man to put it to that test."

Neilson reached into a drawer, took out an electron pistol, slipped the safety ring, and sighted it on Dam.

"I'm calling your bluff, Mister. In five seconds I fire. Convince me, or you're dead."

Dam's hand was already in his pocket and the control button of the pulse unit was hard against his index finger. Nevertheless he waited as long as he dared, until he saw Neilson's eyes harden with intent. Then Dam moved: he achieved para-ion state a full half-second before Neilson had intended to shoot, and the shock of Dam's transition caused Neilson to fire prematurely; the weapon-blast passed straight through Dam's body and shattered the panelling beyond, while Dam launched himself at the suddenly frightened sub-sector, smashed the pistol from his hands, threw him heavily to the floor, and overturned the heavy metal desk on top of him. Before Neilson had had time to work out what had taken place, Dam was back in normal molecular state, and the sub-sector was peering fixedly down the focusing coils of his own electron weapon.

"Convinced, Sub-Sector?" asked Dam. "You were armed, I was not—yet I could have killed you fifty different ways had I chosen."

"I'm convinced!" Neilson struggled painfully out from beneath the desk, examined his bruises, and surveyed the ruins of his office. Then he took back the offered ion pistol and threw it with some disgust into a cupboard. "Para-ion . . ." His hands were still shaking with reactive shock. ". . . I've seen it used in the field with a shipful of equipment as backup, but how the hell . . ."

"Hence the hyper-security tag." Dam offered the soft part of his forearm for Neilson to touch. "Feel the mesh beneath the skin—the para-ion suit is in-built, along with the power supply and the control module. It's the newest para-ion technique, and by far the most deadly."

"Point taken, Assassin Stormdragon. If I'd not seen it with my own eyes, I'd never have believed it possible. My apologies for doubting you."

"You'd not have been doing your job if you hadn't been healthily suspicious," said Dam, "You'll get a commendation in my reports. I too apologise, for having to offer you proof the hard way. But you now realize how imperative it is for the secret to be kept."

"I don't even like to think about it," said Neilson sorely. "And you reckon Liam Liam's to be found on Ampola?"

"It's the best information we have, though it may be only the lead-clue in a long chase. But one thing's certain—I have to stop Liam Liam before he manages to incite the Hub dissidents to unite in all-out war."

Behind his answer, Dam's brain was racing. Neilson had mentioned the name of the planet Ampola, and the only thing he could glean from the context was that Ampola was the fleet's destination. Ampola was in the centre of the Hub territories, and the nearest habitable planet to his homeworld of Castalia. He grasped at the idea with feelings of elation and anger hopelessly intermixed—he could scarcely have expected the luck to be transported so close to the region he was trying to reach, yet the joy was crowded out by the dreadful implications of Terra's intentions towards one of the Hub's most beautiful and civilized worlds.

"Come!" Security Sub-Sector Neilson took him by the arm. "We'll find you quarters with the security detail for the flight, if that's acceptable. Once under-way, I'll arrange a session with the Sector Commander. We'll have to integrate our campaigns most carefully, so that we don't spoil your operation and you don't confuse ours. I'll tell you something, Stormdragon. With your abilities, I'm certain glad you're on our side."

During the journey to the Hub, Dam's constant fear was that some communication over the radio link from Terra would report the incident of the paraformer carrier and the escape of a para-ion warrior with special abilities. Although he took good care to read all the intelligence reports which came into the security unit where he was quartered, no such reports came through, and he was forced to conclude that the corvette which had pursued the pinnace had missed the fact of his tachyon-space leap and interpreted the flare of their own missiles as proof of his destruction.

Sub-Sector Neilson's conviction of his legitimacy now appeared complete, and the ground for Dam's interview with Sector Commander Canwolf had been so carefully prepared that Canwolf himself readily accepted the importance and integrity of the supposed assassin's mission. The meeting mainly explored the ways in which Dam's activities could be aided by the presence of the fleet. Dam played his bluff warily, insisting on absolute autonomy, but asking for a special communications channel to be reserved in case a phase of the operation required the use of fleet backup. He was issued with a radio-communication hot-line direct to the flagship. He had no intention of making use of the facility, but it appeared to be in keeping with the part he was playing, and had a potential use as a means of arranging a diversion should one be required.

When the planetary destination had been reached and the ship ring established in orbit, Dam was taken in a lifecraft over the planet's darkside, and dropped in a space-recovery landfall pod as he had requested. In the tubular-coffin confines of the pod he was overcome by an immense tide of relief at being finally away from the Terrans and heading towards his own kind; yet he was simultaneously sad and angry, because even from the immense height at which the pod had been slipped out of orbit he could distinctly see through the faceport the blaze of exploding space-bombs where the orbiting fleet had chosen to treat some of the 'dissidents' to a foretaste of the power of Terran colonial control.

CHAPTER XXVII

Space-recovery pods, because of their brief operational life-spans, were not normally equipped with radio communications. A short-lived chemical oxygen cartridge, a measure of heat insulation, an outer husk to be burnt off by atmospheric friction during re-entry, two space-chutes, an altimeter and a retro landing rocket were the sum total of the assets with which the man-bearing cylinder was equipped. These facilities were a bare survival minimum, and fatalities resulting from the use of such pods were many; but for Dam, who needed a quiet way to make planetfall in advance of the Terran occupation forces, the risk had seemed worth while, especially with the use of a lifecraft to put him in the precise trajectory to make a theoretically safe descent.

Unlike the usual survivor of a space disaster, however, Dam additionally had the hot-line communications pack hung from his neck in front of him, and was still able to communicate with the flagship whose lifecraft had cast him into space. Shortly after the free descent began, the operator at the ship end had been replaced by Sub-Sector Neilson, who had followed his departure with great interest.

"How are you faring, Assassin Stormdragon? All is well, I trust?"

"As a way of life, descent by space-pod leaves much to be desired."

"I know what you mean," said Neilson. "I only once had the misfortune to make such a descent, and I'll never forget it. That's why I decided to make it easier for you."

"Easier?" Dam sensed an undercurrent in the security chief's voice. "How?"

Neilson's voice was calm, but there was a cold edge of anticipation. "You see, my dear Assassin, I had one of the space-chutes removed from your pod."

"You did what!"

"I just told you. Do you know what happens to a pod with only one effective chute? It enters the lower atmosphere too fast—not fast enough to burn it away completely, but sufficient to generate a fine white heat. Thus you too will carry the impressions for the rest of your life . . . only the time scale has been reduced from years to minutes."

"Are you mad?"

"No, my Hub friend. But I would have been mad if I'd believed you."

"I don't understand."

"I asked you if you expected to find Liam Liam on Ampola. You immediately assumed Ampola to be our destination, and have been speaking that way ever since. But it was a trick question. We were never scheduled for Ampola, and that's not Ampola towards which you are now falling. What kind of espionage agent is it who doesn't know where he's supposed to be going?"

"Hell! If you thought I was bluffing, you gave remarkably little hint of it."

"Then you'll remember giving me a demonstration of your prowess. It was a lesson I marked well. Frankly, with those abilities you'd have had no difficulty in taking over the whole ship had you felt menaced. That was a risk neither I nor the sector commander was prepared to take. Better to wait until you'd left the ship of your own accord—and then arrange your destruction in a way which makes even your talents powerless. Strange as it may seem to you, we Terrans are not the fools you imagine us to be."

"I try never to underestimate the opposition. And I advise you not to do so either. Your campaign against the Hub is a war you can't possibly win."

Dam switched off the communicator pack as the pod entered the tenuous outer atmosphere of the planet towards which he was falling. The frictional heat produced by his passage through even such a rarefied gas was plainly raising the temperature of the husk to white heat. As Neilson had predicted, the pod would not burn out completely, but would continue to descend on one chute at so rapid a rate that when the disposable burn-off husk was completely gone, the pod itself would proceed to overheat—and there was no possible route by which he might escape from the metal tube soon to be raised a thousand degrees Celsius above human tolerance.

He considered firing the retro rocket prematurely, but realized this would provide only a temporary palliative, and that his present height was sufficient to permit the regaining of a crucifying velocity long after the retro had burned and gone. Additionally, he would have lost the facility of being able to check his ground-approach speed assuming he reached that far without prior cremation. He watched with a fascinated fear as the great flames of the burnout of the husk began to rush past the faceplate and completely outshine the illumination from the spacebombs falling on the planet beneath. Then the husk was mainly gone, and he felt the interior heat beginning to build up. A little sector of the wall, more exposed than the rest, began to assume a cherry redness, accompanied by the overpowering stench of singed paint and cables as his life-support system itself began to be destroyed by the ever-rising temperature of the fragile little hull.

The glowing redness of the fragment of the wall turned Dam's mind instantly to two of Absolute's training exercises: firstly the sessions on the furnace environent; and secondly, the ability of the para-ion energy shell to withstand pressures which would have completely destroyed a molecular body. If survival was possible in his situation, it was so only in para-ion state. Already he could feel his uniform begin to singe, and the atmosphere was becoming impossible to breathe. He pressed the actuator button on the pulse unit in his pocket, and his body adopted the identity of the crude atmosphere in which he was immersed. He made the transition not a second too soon, because the chemical oxygen supply-candle took fire, and the free liberation of the gas caused a hot steel strut section to explode with a shower of white-hot sparks that would have burned his legs away had he not been in para-ion form.

Inside his mini-hell Dam grew increasingly apprehensive about his impact velocity. The exterior of the pod itself was now beginning to burn off, and the walls had risen to a bright red heat. The external flames were streaming past the face-plate to an extent which made it impossible for him to see anything at all of the night-side of the world towards which he was rushing, and the altimeter had long since ceased to function. His agonized mental debate as to precisely when he should fire the retro-rocket, however, was terminated by the decision being taken from him. Housed in a casting taken to a temperature beyond the tolerance of the propellant inside, the retro rocket fired itself. The flaming backwash wrapped the tortured little structure in a sparkling silver fireball.

Such was the efficiency of the super-heated retro rocket in checking the pod's velocity, that the weakened metal walls actually bulged with the sudden force of the checked momentum, and Dam felt unseen pressures crushing his para-ion form down against the leading end of the pod. Then the rocket was spent, and again he was in free-fall, and to judge from the tearing whine of the atmosphere against the hull he was still travelling far too fast for even his para-ion energy shell to survive when he smashed into the ground.

Finally came the impact which he had been dreading; he was hopelessly compressed by the sudden crowding force which smashed him downwards at the same time as his ears were being smitten by a scream which he could associate only as being a demon chorus straight from Hell. So grossly was his energy shell distorted that his brain imposed a protective blanket of unconsciousness to ward off the unendurable level of pain, and Dam slipped into a tide of blackness which engulfed him hungrily like the opening of some strange mouth.

He awoke to find himself in a metal-confined blackness that had a slight suggestion of a rhythmic rise and fall. The pod had plunged into some deep water which had considerably cushioned its fall and quenched its meteoric heat. Even so, the drastic shock to the overheated metal had caused it to fracture in places, and although the pod was floating upright, the occasional wavetips splashing through a split across the top warned him that he had little time.

The faint milky-whiteness of the faceplate suggested the possible imminence of dawn on whatever planet it was on which he had arrived, and this forced Dam to consider his alternatives. The pod would remain afloat longer if he did not attempt to open the hatch, but if opening the distorted metal was to prove as difficult as he feared, there was a real chance of shipping enough water to sink the assembly before he could escape. On the other hand he could apply himself to the hatch immediately, and attempt to swim his way clear of the gallant little pod, but at the risk of finding himself in darkness in the middle of an unnamed ocean, with only his swimming endurance to buoy him.

An unusually heavy rush of water through the fracture cautioned Dam that his options were purely relative, and that the sea was his main enemy whichever course he chose. Dam was certain the external unit would short out if immersed in water. He therefore reverted to normal molecular identity and began to struggle with the hatch. Fortunately the space-alloy had had its temper drawn by the fierce heat of its journey, and additionally, the parts had suffered considerable oxidation. Aided by a growing desperation, Dam finally managed to break away the hatch rather than open it, and, fighting the flooding waters, he was able to swim clear after being carried only a short way beneath the surface.

Gasping for breath, he attempted to look about him. The light he had assumed was dawn was not the coming of the sun but the illumination from great star-clusters ranked across the perfect velvet of the sky. Such was the level of the star-glow that his imagination could paint distant coastlines or unbroken sea wherever he looked and depending on the hopefulness of his mood. Realistically he could determine no reason to swim in one direction rather than another, and could as easily proceed away from potential safety as towards it. Then Dam noticed a hint of light—a single point on the horizon whose distance he could not determine. The portent of this solitary beacon was beyond all calculation, but whether it represented ship or shore was irrelevant. Kicking his shoes off, Dam began to swim towards the light.

Dam was a powerful swimmer; he'd spent a large part of his childhood exploring the canals and water-courses around his native water-forest. Nevertheless the journey taxed him to the utmost. For a long time he seemed to be making no progress at all, and feared he might be in the grip of a powerful current. However, with the gradual coming of morning he found himself at the entrance to a broad, natural bay; the light which had beckoned him was a beacon astride a white tower marking the entrance to what appeared to be a small navigable river. He found, too, that there was a bank nearer than the light itself. With rapidly fading strength he altered his course and made towards the nearest shore, finally wading through the line of clement breakers to collapse exhausted on a strand of fine white sand.

CHAPTER XXVIII

Dam awoke to a clear sky and a brilliant sun, yet possessed by an urgent sense of danger he was unable to define. Something, a noise perhaps, had penetrated his sleep and triggered an internal alarm. Yet as he stood up on the warming sands and began to search about, he could see nothing threatening. Suddenly there were specks on the horizon and instantly Dam was flat on his face hugging the ground as a dozen pilotless Terran cruise-drones, travelling as about Mach three and barely a hundred meters up, bulleted in from the direction of the sea and passed virtually overhead. The blast of their jets provoked a brief sandstorm along the beach, and the concussive shockwave of their passing smote him a great blow on the back which made his chest cavity ring. As swiftly as they had come, the missiles were gone out of his sight beyond the bank. As their engine noise drained from the skies the great silence which followed seemed absolute.

Dam stayed on the ground until he was sure the drones were not going to explode in his immediate vicinity, then struggled up with a heavy heart. He was reasonably sure now that what had first awakened him had been a previous flight of drones passing a little further along the coast. All would have been injected from space by a Terran weapon-ship, and each would contain a warhead of ultra-powerful explosive sufficient not only to shatter a town but to literally pulverize it. Such weapons would be brought down on strategic sites near major population centres, and, cannily guarded by unbeat-able triggers, would await the space-signal to de-struct. Thus whole populations or selected areas could be destroyed at a whim, and the 'sins' of the 'dissidents' could be avenged wherever and whenever expedience dictated. The Terrans were running true to form.

Having learned from Sub-Sector Neilson that this world was not Ampola, Dam was already searching for clues as to which Hub planet he was on. Training visits in the Space Army had given him some famil-iarity with perhaps a dozen of the Hub worlds, but the sea-scape which surrounded him might have belonged to almost any of them. The fact that the cruise-drones had passed the area was a probable indication of the direction of at least one township, and he followed the general line which the drones had taken as he made his way along the sandy strip. His route took him along the edge of the bay and close to where the white tower carried the light which had guided him ashore.

He found the tower was an automatic, unattended beacon, built on a base of fine white stone that gave no overt clues as to which planetary population had been responsible for its design. In its base was a heavy, locked door, beside which was an alcove harboring what claimed to be a distress alarm for use in emergencies. Dam pressed the button and waited, but neither sea-craft nor flier responded to his call. Finally he shrugged. If he had the feel of the situation aright, the planetary emergency services were already too stretched by the Terran campaign to be able to respond swiftly. An anonymous signal from an isolated coastal point would fall low on a list of desperate priorities.

He turned his attention then to the rocky bank and the countryside beyond. In swimming ashore he had lost his shoes, and his feet were not hardened for barefoot walking over the broken, rocky terrain presented by the bank; nevertheless he struggled painfully up to find himself at the foot of a range of steep hills which cupped the bay in a neatly semi-circular bowl. Still following the approximate direction taken by the cruise-drones, Dam found to his relief that the texture of the hills made for less-painful walking than had the bank, and within an hour he had approached the brow of a hill and was in a position to get his first view of the countryside beyond.

He stopped in amazement as he looked down across water glades and fountain clusters so typical of his own native Castalia. With a little cry of triumph he began to run down the farther slope, drenched in the joy of an unexpected homecoming. Then suddenly he was hugging the ground again and praying, as a further flight of cruise-drones, hugging the contours of the hill, clawed their way a few scant meters above his head, and bulleted across the water glades like terrifying messengers from Hell. Dam knew he was back somewhere on his own world, but felt suddenly empty and sick and angry, because he knew the Terrans' potential for committing gross atrocities against both the population and the environment. His brain was overcome with a peculiar numb terror at the thoughts of what his precious Castalia might become.

Such were the levels of local crisis and his distance from the capital, that it took Dam three days of pleading and argument to obtain the transport necessary to take him to his destination. It would have taken ever longer had he not managed to reach a Space Army outpost and convince the commander of his identity and the seriousness of his mission.

In the course of this liaison he learned of the almost complete acquiescence of the Castalian government to Terran demands, the rapidity with which the indigenous defence forces were being disbanded and their arms destroyed.

The Castalian government had been faced with a simple choice—absolute obedience to Terran orders or the loss of ninety percent of the planetary population within ten hours. There was no point in dying in defence of a world which would become an uninhabitable slag-ball long before the battle could be concluded: better continued existence while looking for a way to remove the crucifying yoke of Terra from their necks.

Once convinced of Dam's story, the commander saw the potential in Dam's para-ion approach, and, although he had no personal knowledge of how Liam Liam might be contacted, he swiftly arranged for Dam to be provided with a dead man's identity papers, inconspicuous civilian clothes, and transport to the vicinity of the township of Darrieus, where Senator Anrouse was located.

On his arrival in Darrieus, Dam was immediately

aware of the Terran presence: formidably-armed shipmen of the occupation fleet patrolled the streets and stood guard on all the important buildings; and it was certain that at least as many plain-clothed men of the security detail were sifting through the township searching for any signs of a possible resistance movement. Martial law had been imposed, with civilian movements severely restricted; and the Terran insistence on obedience was absolute. The crash of electron fire told of the frequent summary executions by which the invaders exercised their spite and enforced their commands. Indeed, the whole township seemed to cringe beneath a blanket of grey apprehension.

Having been set down on the outskirts, Dam made his way on foot through forlorn streets. Beneath the shapeless jacket with which he had been provided, he carried a heavy-duty electron pistol and the pulse unit which controlled his para-ion identity. He was careful to avoid any check-points at which a personal search might be involved; he had no intention of allowing himself to be searched, and the Terran unit which attempted such a feat was due for swift destruction. But he was mindful of the terrible retribution such an incident could bring to the local population.

To contact Anrouse, he went not to the government buildings, which he knew would be heavily guarded, but instead worked his way towards the chambers used by the senator when attending to his official duties in Darrieus. There appeared to be no Terrans in the vicinity, and a letter given to him by the commander of the Space Army outpost took him neatly through Anrouse's own guards and into the presence of one of the Senator's aides. When the man realized who Dam was, he paled visibly.

"You should have known better than to come here, Stormdragon. Your presence could kill us all should the Terrans learn you are here."

"Thanks for the welcome-home," Dam replied drily, "but I take your point. I came to see Senator Anrouse because he's the only route I know to Liam Liam."

"I think you mistake the Senator's connection with the Hub revolutionary." The aide was being deliberately guarded.

"Perhaps. But it was Absolute Anrouse who sent me."

"Absolute?" The aide's brow clouded with confusion. Then he came to a sudden decision. "Wait here. I'll see if the Senator will see you."

Dam was shortly shown into an upstairs room where Anrouse was sitting at a desk leafing through piles of papers. He stopped when Dam entered and rose to shake hands. He had aged incredibly since last they had met; his voice was that of a tired and fragile man. The aide remained with them in the room, watching his principal with concern.

"We thought you were dead, Dam," said Anrouse gravely. "And Absolute, too. By now you'll have worked out for yourself why you were sent. Where's Absolute?"

"I last saw her on a ship on the outskirts of the Solar system. Liam Liam, I think made a rescue attempt which failed. So I've come in her place, with information Liam needs."

"What sort of information?"

"Have you heard about the para-ion suit beneath the skin? I have that capability."

"Liam sent word to me about it after the Syman affair. But you come too late, Dam. Liam's base is a long haul from Castalia, and the Terrans have left us no means of getting either ship or message through to it. For that matter Liam himself may be dead. The last news we received was that he had been trapped during an engagement near Sol, perhaps that was the same incident as the one you mentioned."

"I was there," said Dam. "But I didn't see the end of the action. They could well have escaped."

Anrouse shook his head sadly, and retired behind his desk. "I suspect that's an exercise in wishful thinking. Certainly Liam's ship was forced to return with him, and from the lack of opposition to the Terran's approach to Castalia, we can only fear the worst. Which brings us back to the realities of your own situation."

"Senator?"

"For all our sakes, get lost, Dam! Put down your arms, fade into the background—and stay there. Do nothing to cause the Terrans to become aware of your existence—else they'll carve up half the planet just to ensure you don't survive. Do I make myself clear?"

"Perfectly clear, Senator." Dam tried without success to restrain the tide of bitterness which rose in his voice. "But I came back to Castalia to fight, not to hide."

"Then you know nothing at all about the real nature of bravery, Stormdragon." Anrouse was suddenly the larger-than-life character he had always seemed, and his voice burst across the room like the explosion of a bomb.

"I don't see what you mean."

"If you reveal your privileged hand against the Terrans, in return they'll slaughter millions and poison these lands for all eternity. That is where your 'bravery' would lead us. Far better that you find a quiet corner and turn your weapons against yourself. You're a danger to Castalia, Dam. Your presence represents a catalyst which could unleash the most unholy reaction of them all."

CHAPTER XXIX

Dam, however, had ceased to listen. The growing noise of vehicles in the street outside cautioned him that something new was happening, and the sharp rasp of instructions told that a Terran raid was in progress. Anrouse and his aide were clearly aware of the noises, too, and Dam felt that both men were caught up in a web of tension. Down in the hallway below there was a sudden crash as the main door was thrown open, followed by the sound of men entering, and of several sharp demands. Anrouse was looking at his aide, and there was bitter accusation on his face. Dam, also, followed the chain of cause and event through to its logical conclusion.

"You bastard! You sold me to the Terrans!"

"Only to buy a little time," said the aide sincerely. "Believe me, time is the thing Castalia needs most."

He had produced a pistol and levelled it at Dam. Gambling that it was the fellow's intention to hold him immobile rather than to kill, Dam's hand continued to move towards his pocket. He hit the para-ion actuator button through the cloth of his jacket, and it responded instantly. Even as he blended into para-ion identity he was drawing his ion pistol, but it was a burst of fire from Anrouse himself which actually killed the aide. Almost immediately, the door burst open and a trained arrest squad called on Dam to emerge without offering resistance. He emerged, but not as they had hoped. His para-ion form leaped from the room to the centre of the hallway, and, oblivious to their frenetic weapon-fire, he turned with his electron pistol and cut down every member of the arrest squad, then took the stairs in a single bound and wrought gross havoc among a group of the Terran military waiting below. Still firing wildly at everyone in sight, he broke out into the startled street, but not before he had seen Anrouse's head appear over the balusters, looking white with apprehension. Even in the white heat of the moment, Dam managed to throw him a brief salute.

In the roadway he chose the nearest vehicle, gunned down the crew, and flung their bodies out of his way. His heavy-duty electron pistol exploded the engines of the three remaining vehicles, two of which immediately took fire. Dam brought his own vehicle to life and urged it to a ferocious speed to shatter a hastily improvised road-block being moved into his path. The crew erecting the road-block went down like skittles under his murderous approach, and the barriers they had placed across the highway were scattered forcibly against the buildings on either side. Before reinforcements could arrive he was through, weaving a tortuous course not along the thoroughfares as might have been expected, but down towards Darrieus's edge, where the tangle of wharves and bridges denoted the presence of the canals and water-courses which formed the main commercial links with the other inland towns.

By the time the Terran searchers had located the vehicle, it had been abandoned; and there was no way of telling down which of several adjacent roads their quarry might have fled, or whether, indeed, he had escaped by water down one of the branches of the canal. Perhaps because the whole incident reflected badly on the competence of the Terran occupation force, a full report never reached the Sector Commander in orbit, and reprisals were relatively slight. Meanwhile, a traveller had returned to his old home at the edge of the Water Forest, and was engaged in a serious consideration of what his next move ought to be.

His house had been virtually abandoned since the time that Dam had left for Terra with Colonel Dimede, although one of the watermen had been engaged to see to its repair and keep the water-gardens neatened and well stocked. On a stolen sled, throttled down to pass with the merest turbine whisper, Dam had returned to the house and carefully contrived to enter in such a way that his presence could not be known even to an observer who knew the ways of the water-folk. He was greatly disturbed, therefore, when he was awakened in the strange twilight between second and first-light by the arrival of another sled, which tied-up on the landing steps. The single occupant of the sled searched the quiet water wastes carefully before knocking quietly on Dam's door.

"Ho Stormdragon! It is I, Marke Sten."

Dam's finger relaxed on the trigger, but he kept

the weapon raised as he carefully unlocked the door. Marke Sten was a senior water-guide and an old friend, but Dam had already learned the hard way that the old values could not be relied upon. In the near-darkness Marke acknowledged the presence of the weapon with open hands.

"Peace, Dam! I don't blame you being careful, but I'm unarmed. Search me if you like."

"How did you know I was back?"

Sten gestured. "Nobody uses the waterways without the watermen knowing. That's the message that brings me here. The Terrans have put a large price on your head, and there are a few who'll attempt to claim it. I warn you, Dam, this is no place for you to rest."

"Thanks for the warning, Marke. If you found me so quickly, then others won't be very far behind. What's the answer?"

"Come with me. I'll take you to a safer place."

Dam's finger tightened imperceptibly on the trigger.

"Where to?"

"To friends. Long before the Terrans actually attacked, we were reading the signs. There's a resistance organization called Free Castalia. They'll have need of you."

"I need to contact Liam Liam or those who take his place."

"I know nothing of them, but if there is a way, our friends will probably be best placed to find it."

"That makes sense. But you'll excuse my wariness. Already I've been betrayed once in Darrieus. How can I be sure this isn't another trap?"

"You can't be sure, except that you know me of old. But you'd best not delay the decision. I can hear engines in the watercourse."

Listening carefully, Dam, too, could hear the muted drone far to his left, in the direction of the channels leading to the river. Their coming might have been a coincidence, but such a concentration of night craft was sufficiently unusual to cause him to make the connection which Sten had already made. With a sudden gesture he thrust the pistol back into his jacket and offered the waterman his hand.

"Let's get out of here! What time does the Water Forest rise?"

"It's already rising. By the time we reach the groves the trees will be nearly full. A thousand men could hide there and none of them be found until the waters subside."

Marke Sten started his turbines and held the craft against the post until Dam had leaped aboard, then he drove the sled at such a speed that only his masterful piloting prevented it from capsizing. Within minutes of this furious pace they were lost from sight amongst the boles of the liquid trees. Scarcely had they become thus obscured when Dam's house burst into a great gout of flame which lit the Water Forest with a fiery redness which the fountains had never before known.

Dam could have sworn that he himself knew every water passage and channel intimately, but as they cleared the far end of the forest he knew he was outclassed. With a precision which left no possible margin for error, Sten set the speeding sled straight at the rivulet-punctuated banks of the marshes beyond. Twisting and turning the craft as though it was a living thing, he struck sufficient water every time between the reeded banks, and thus progressed at a continuingly furious pace through a region of banks and broken water which most would have sworn unnavigable. Then they broke through to the dark waters of a canal beyond, and thence to a river, where heavy vessels of seagoing ilk rose starkly black amid a treacherous jungle of anchor chains and buoys.

Here, amid the tangle of piers and wharves, Sten turned the craft suddenly into a narrow, brick-lined channel which terminated soon at the foot of a flight of steps. He steadied the sled while Dam leaped out, then, in the growing colours of first-light, he gravely saluted his farewell.

"Here's as far as I go, Dam. Someone will meet you above. Take care of yourself, and may God give fortune to your hand in battle!"

The little sled spun within its own length in the water and was gone. Dam ensured the safety ring on his pistol was slipped, then carefully ascended the worn stone of the steps. A lone figure was waiting for him against the rail at the road's edge, and among the line of sleeping houses one solitary door was marked by an edge of light. Dam was motioned through and found himself in a room with the cosy, trim utility of a typical waterman's cottage. The three people in the room, two women and a man, were joined by the fellow who had met Dam in the street, and the drapes were again drawn against outside observation.

"Welcome you to Free Castalia, Dam Stormdragon! We know of you, but you don't know us. We're a cell of the Castalian Liberation Army; we extend to you an invitation to join our ranks."

Dam's eyes were summing the occupants of the room. All were gripped by the same drama of the occasion, yet none of them looked to have had actual fighting experience. His reluctant conclusion was that he had fallen into the hands of a group of well-intentioned amateurs.

"What do you know of me?" was his guarded question.

"You've a commission in the Space Army." One of the women, whose name had been given as Baba was ticking off items on her fingers. "You're trained in all branches of weaponry; you're a qualified aerospace pilot, you've seen tithe service with the Terran fleet; and you currently head the list of men most wanted by the Terran pigs. That makes you something of a celebrity."

"More to the point, it also makes me something of a liability. You'll have problems enough with anonymity on your side."

"Then you won't help us?" Jorg Turgen, the man who had met Dam in the street, eyed him anxiously.

"I would rather ask if you can help me. I've an urgent need to contact Liam Liam's organization. I've information they need to carry the war directly against the orbiting fleet—or even back to Terra if the chance arises. I see this as being more to the point than trying to fight the battle on Castalia itself. Twist the Terrans tails too hard, and they'll sterilize the planet. Only in space can they actually be beaten."

"What sort of help would you need?" asked Baba.

"I know nothing of the whereabouts of Liam Liam, except that he has a base within the Hub. Do you have any communications channels which can reach other worlds?"

Turgen shrugged. "We've secret access to a commercial FTL link, but the Terrans are jamming the entire transmission spectrum."

"That we can break, by sending repetitive transmissions at fixed time intervals. The original signal can then be separated from the jamming noise by coincidence sensing. The problem is where to direct the beam. Have any of you a clue in which direction Liam's base might be located?"

Suddenly the man who had not yet spoken bound to his feet with a finger raised in urgent caution. He killed the lights in the room and moved to the window, peering carefully around the corners of the heavy drapes.

"I thought as much!" His face was white with anxiety. "Terran patrols at both ends of the street. They may be coming here."

"Quickly! Through the back way," said Turgen, indicating a small door to the rear. "There's an alley leading out to the river path."

There was a sudden flurry of near-panic as the conspirators made for the little door; but just before they reached it the door itself was smashed from its hinges by the force of a great blow struck from the outside, and the startled group were staring straight into the carbon-blackened coils of well-used Terran weapons and into the hard eyes of the uniformed men who held them.

"Anyone who moves is dead," a voice informed them. "Most especially lover-boy here, who would be doubly dead before he could reach halfway to his para-ion control. So nobody moves a single muscle until your weapons are removed and Stormdragon has been neutralized. I have little time for games, you understand?''

CHAPTER XXX

As the pinnace leaped from Castalia, the officer in charge searched Dam's unhappy face with a slightly sardonic smile on his lips.

"Welcome back, lover-boy! You didn't really think we'd let talents like yours escape us? You don't realize how valuable you are."

Dam spat expressively. "Not to you, I'm not. There's no way you can force me to fight on your behalf."

The officer shook his head ruefully. "You're wrong there, my lecherous Hub friend. When I tell you fight, you will fight. I have methods of persuasion, you understand?"

"They won't help you. Let me get back into para-ion identity and I swear I'll turn your own weapons against you."

"We shall see!"

Having gained orbital height, the pinnace headed not for the flagship, as Dam had expected, but far out to where a craft he identified as a paraformer mother-ship was separately located. Dam was reasonably sure no such vessel had accompanied the fleet, and surmised it must have been a later addition. It was only when they had closed for docking that Dam realized it was the selfsame carrier from which he had escaped near Sol. The fact baffled him slightly, because he was sure insufficient time had elapsed for the carrier to have reached Terra, acquired a second paraforming ship, and then travelled to Castalia's orbit. He was even more surprised on boarding to find a second paraforming craft securely installed on the ramps.

Then he stopped, relief building in his face: and suddenly he was laughing as the true nature of the monstrous joke flooded his comprehension with a rare and uncontrollable joy. The mad-bright stare of the shipman who hurried to release his bonds could have belonged to none other than Fiendish; and the other members of the para-ion squad captured on Syman were there as well. Also there was a second para-ion squad, all new faces to Dam, but obviously men from the Hub and of the toughest fighting grade that he could imagine. Lastly, there was Absolute, triumphant fire in her eyes, and a look of confident determination which could have routed an army. Her delight at seeing him blazed like a beacon, and the warmth of their re-union evoked a great cheer of admiration from the assembled onlookers.

Shortly the man who had posed as a Terran officer tapped Dam on the shoulder.

"You are not to eat her, you understand? I hate to break up a dedicated clinch, but I've a war to run, and my Castalian sources suggested you were looking for me."

"You're Liam Liam? Yes, you have to be Liam! Nobody else would dare operate so closely within the Terran fleet."

"The weakness of bureaucracy is that it encourages abuse by those unscrupulous enough to play the system against itself. But the time for compliments must wait. Our battle tactics are laid, with Absolute and yourself as key components. Did I not say I had means of persuading you to fight?"

In far orbit the Terran hellship was observing the approaching pinnace with some interest: visitors to the ship were rare and always provided a measure of relief from the lonely monotony of manning the most feared and isolated ship in the whole fleet. Slumbering uneasily in the hellship's cooled and insulated bays were seven of the deadliest weapons ever devised, each with the inherent stability of a carboy of nitroglycerine on a hot tin roof. This fact was sufficient to ensure that visitors seldom came without the excellent reason.

The interest of the hellship's crew was heightened even more when the docked pinnace disembarked a female officer whose trim looks and magnetic personality negated the security counter-check requirements and led her straight to a comfortable chair in the captain's cabin. Five seconds after the cabin door had closed, however, the captain was dead, and the para-ion person who emerged was a female of a more literally fatal kind. Before the hellship's crew had come to fully appreciate her nature, their phantom visitor had destroyed both radio room and occupants with bursts of electron fire, and was busy attacking the environmental controls which helped keep the hellburners quiescent.

Some of the crewmen tried to cut her down with hand weapons, but their fire was completely ineffective. Others, in an agony of panic, took to the life-craft, only to be neatly taken out of space by marksmen in the pinnace, which had backed-off and was obviously waiting for them. Then at a signal the pinnace returned to the hellship, picked up its ghostly saboteur, and began a hasty return to the lower orbits where the main fleet remained unaware of what had taken place. The pinnace had just managed to regain the carrier when the hellship exploded, and this was a fortunate circumstance for the crew because all seven hellburners triggered simultaneously to create a burst of deadly heat and radiation which began to tax the best shields in the fleet.

The explosion of the hellship caused a wave of dismay to run through the fleet. In one hectic fraction of a second there had been stripped from them the ultimate threat which they had contrived to hang over Castalia. Their concern was not made less by the failure of the sector commander to reply to the urgent requests for instructions which flooded his communications terminal. His failure to respond would have been better understood had it been known that Sector Commander Canwolf was already dead from a burst of electron fire. His body lay alongside that of Sub-Sector Neilson who had been similarly treated by the weapons of an officer, who, having been admitted to the flagship on forged credentials, had inexplicably converted to the para-ion condition.

Having robbed the fleet of their commander, the ghost warrior's next move had been to destroy the communications room in order to prevent broadcast alarms being sent to the rest of the fleet. So swiftly did he accomplish this task that the communications men were actually unaware of a crisis on board their vessel until both they and their equipment were shattered and burned. Then the deadly phantom, cutting down anyone who dared stand in his path, leaped down several companion-ways to the engineering section to gain control of the motor boards and to so expertly disable the flight controls that the flagship entered an unalterable descent spiral towards the planet which would bring it certain incineration as it entered the atmosphere at terminal velocity.

Except for this last action, the attack on the flagship had been accomplished in such a way that observers in the other ships would have had no visual indication that anything was wrong. Dam's return to the pinnace, however, was the signal for a new phase of the operation to begin. With the flagship nosing ever more heavily towards drastic burn-up, groups of Liam's para-ion men, using both paraformer ships and a couple of pinnaces, managed to gain access to four of the fleet corvettes. Having disposed of the crews, they swiftly took over the automatic gunnery systems and emptied the ships' entire armouries of target-seeking missiles into the orbital paths of the warfleet. They followed this action by liberating over two thousand space mines into the nearer approaches before setting the corvettes' powerplants to run critical and escaping back into space in their small ships.

Liam's plan had been the deliberate creation of chaos. Having had the fleet's commander struck down, and broken the communications chain at several points, he now focused on intensifying the growing panic in the fleet. The *Starbucket*, out in deep-space, began to mimic the Terran Command FTL transmission, broadcasting a warning to the Castalian orbital fleet of an armed mutiny within their own ranks. With the space-approaches bright with the flare of target-seeking missiles and treacherous with mines all released from Terran ships, many captains needed no further evidence to convince them of the truth of the report, and proceeded to fire on any vessel close enough to pose an active threat. Thus Terran guns came increasingly to bear on Terran ships, and even some of those too well shielded to succumb to weapon-fire or projectiles still fell to the magnetic attentions of the space-mines.

Their panic and confusion was tuned to new heights when a great number of unidentified spacecraft spread out of tachyon space on the fringes of the conflict, wrought great havoc among the mazed fleetships, then leaped back into tachyon space almost before the automatic weapon systems of the fleet had been able to plot their brief trajectories. The punch of the weapons delivered by these infuriatingly vanishing craft ripped great holes in the fabric of the fleet and shattered the morale of the men still further as it became apparent that the Terran force was due for a crushing defeat. Rallying now against a common and obvious enemy, the Terran ships attempted to re-group. However, this proved to be a great mistake as concealed missile silos on Castalia itself began to open-up with massive shipbreakers which even the best protected of ships could not withstand.

Finally, in space-approaches thickly seeded with mines and treacherous with debris, most of the remainder of the Terran fleet responded to Liam's demand for unconditional surrender. Those units which attempted to escape into deep-space encountered a new sort of ship-chain composed of the unmarked ships of Liam's war, heavily reinforced by vengeful volunteer ships which, breaking tithe-loan conditions, had streaked back towards Castalia anxious to assist in the ending of Terra's colonial rule.

Back on the *Starbucket,* Liam Liam was nodding sagely as the reports of the collapse of the Terran fleet piled high on his desk. Then he turned to Dam and Absolute, who had been asked to join him.

"This doesn't mean we've won, you understand? None of us, least of all the worlds of the Hub, can afford an all-out interstellar war. Therefore we've a need to be more subtle and make full use of our advantages."

"How do you mean?" asked Dam.

"We plan to carry the fight back to Sol and Terra, with para-ion attacks on strategic solar installations and on the surface of Terra itself. Once the destruction comes closer home, our sick mother-planet will be forced to have new thoughts about the megalomaniacs who drive her. Thus we reach towards the cause of the malady rather than battling with the symptoms. But the main burden of this will fall on just the two of you, you understand?"

"Why us in particular?" Dam asked.

Liam glanced at Absolute. "You tell him," he said, with a wry grimace.

"Because, Lover, they've chickened out," said Absolute witheringly. "Despite what we've demonstrated about the advantages of the in-built para-ion technique, something called ethics forbids them doing to others that which has been done to us.

They're going to remain with the old suit system until Wing Ai's labs can come up with something new. That leaves us two of a kind, unique and indispensable, to spearhead the fight against Terra.''

"That's the truth of it, you understand?'' said Liam Liam. "The question is, how soon are you prepared to start?''

Dam's eyes met Absolute's, and the spark which passed between them flared like a nova born in the cramped stuffiness of Liam's little stateroom.

"About after the honeymoon is over, I should think,'' said Dam.